I0679429

DEDICATION

In loving memory of
Officer Thomas Hayes

STRAIGHT FISH

A CORRECTIONAL OFFICER'S STORY
A NOVEL OF LIFE BEHIND BARS

MIKE KNOX

Straight Fish, A Novel
Copyright © 2015 by Mike Knox

All rights reserved. No part of this publication may be
reproduced, stored in a retrieval system, or transmitted,
in any form or by any means, electronic, mechanical,
photocopying, recording, or otherwise, without
the prior written permission of the publisher.
Published in the United States of America.

Cover designed by Stravinski Pierre and Siori Kitajima
for SFAppWorks LLC
www.sfappworks.com
Cover illustration by Stravinski Pierre
Formatting by Siori Kitajima and Ovidiu Vlad,
SFAppWorks LLC
E-book formatted by Ovidiu Vlad

Cataloging-in-Publication data for this book
is available from the Library of Congress

ISBN-13: 978-0-9862679-8-7
ISBN-10: 0986267988

Published by The Sager Group LLC
www.TheSagerGroup.Net
info@TheSagerGroup.Net

STRAIGHT FISH

A CORRECTIONAL OFFICER'S STORY
A NOVEL OF LIFE BEHIND BARS
MIKE KNOX

THE SAGER GROUP

Artifex Te Aduva

This is a work of fiction. Any resemblance to actual, factual people, places, or events is purely a coincidence.

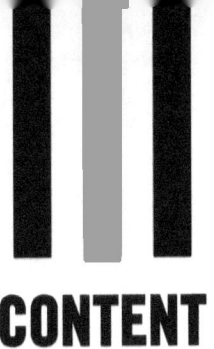

CONTENT

1

MAN DOWN

Attention Staff:
A Federal appeals panel will reconsider its ruling that inmates have a right to mail their semen to artificially inseminate their loved ones. The judge has stated that inmates will be allowed to procreate from prison.

t was a Friday night. I jerked awake and sat up in bed as a sharp pain suddenly shot through my left arm straight into my heart. I had fallen asleep while my wife Natalia lay next to me watching the ten o'clock news. My arm went numb. I massaged it repeatedly with my right hand, trying to circulate the blood. My chest felt like there was a weight holding it down. My heart pounded like it was going to explode. I touched my forehead; I was sweating. The intense pain radiated across my shoulders and neck. I didn't want to tell my wife that I felt scared. This wasn't the first time I had had chest pains, but this was far more intense. I didn't want to admit to anyone that I thought I was having a heart attack. I had always had a high pain threshold. My dentist had even commented on it when he yanked my wisdom teeth six months earlier.

Natalia leaned over and touched my forehead. "Are you all right?" she asked.

"I think so..."

"You look pale."

"I just need some aspirin."

Natalia was worried. "I've never seen you like this. Are you sure you're okay?"

"My chest hurts."

"Do you think it's a heart attack?" Natalia asked, more concerned.

"I think I'm dying."

"Do you want me to call 911?"

The pain was so bad I felt like crying. "Yes," I groaned.

Natalia took the phone off the nightstand and dialed 911. It was busy. We both knew I'd die waiting for an ambulance.

"I'll drive you."

"Okay."

"Do you think you can make it to the car?"

"I think so."

Natalia walked around to the other side of the bed and helped me up. My legs felt like dead weights. I slowly shuffled downstairs and into the car.

It was raining lightly as Natalia drove to the hospital. It was the first rain of November; Thanksgiving was a week away. I thought about my family, and not being around to spend the holidays with them if I died. I struggled to breathe. My lungs felt like they'd collapse at any moment. I rolled down the window and leaned my head out like a sick dog. Natalia was just as scared as I was. We drove in utter silence. She kept her hand on my knee trying to comfort me.

The emergency room was crowded. Natalia yelled at the woman behind the glass. "Pick up the phone and tell them he's having a heart attack!"

A nurse opened a door and we were rushed inside. A second nurse sat me down on a hospital bed. Another nurse put an oxygen mask over my face and stuck an IV in my arm. My shirt was cut open in order to place ten electrocardiograph strips on my chest. A doctor arrived moments later.

"What seems to be the problem?"

"I think I'm having a heart attack."

The doctor stuck a stethoscope to my chest. Then checked my pulse.

"Is it a heart attack?" I asked.

"I don't know."

"It has to be."

"How old are you?

"I'm thirty."

"Have you been doing any drugs?"

"No."

"Drinking alcohol?"
"No."
"Are you on any medications?"
"No."
"It looks like stress."
"I feel like I'm dying!"
"Is there anything stressful in your life right now?"
I looked over at Natalia.
"No."
"What do you do for a living?"
"I'm a prison guard."
He lowered the stethoscope and laughed. "That's your problem right there."

2

THE TOUGHEST BEAT IN THE STATE

Attention Union Members:
In the next few weeks you will receive your mail ballot for the proposed union contract. As the final language is being written, there are many forces at work spreading misinformation and outright lies regarding what is contained or not contained in the contract. We have negotiated pay raises for officers at $74,000 yearly. Please rest assured that prior to casting your vote you will have ample time to read the entire proposal for yourself.

Correctional Officer Henry Bates took my driver's license at the main gate with an empty look, licking his frosted doughnut. He was sweating, even though it was cold out. His gut hung over his utility belt. His nickname around the prison was Officer "Master" Bates, because he had exposed himself to the warden's secretary. Rather than fire Officer Bates, the warden placed him at the front gate as punishment.

As a new correctional officer, I expected some kind of recognition, a hint of camaraderie.

"Where's your state identification?" he demanded. In between bites he gasped for air, managing to spit a few flecks of chocolate icing on the arm I had resting out my car window.

"I'm new. They haven't given it to me."

"Aw, you mean you're another straight fish?" he scoffed.

'Fish' was prison slang for a new officer. A 'straight fish' was a brand-new officer who didn't know shit. It was the worst insult anyone could direct at an officer. It stood for "Fucking Idiot Shit Head."

"See these hash marks on my sleeve?" Officer Bates pointed to five yellow stripes on the left forearm of his uniform.

"Yeah, I see them."

"Each one of these hash marks represents three years. That means I got fifteen years in the department, and you ain't got dick. You don't even know enough to say you don't know anything. How old are you?"

"Twenty-seven."

"The inmates are going to have a lot of fun jacking off to you." He coughed, choking on the last bite of his doughnut. He pressed a button and the wooden gate arm of the guard shack rose, allowing me to drive forward.

It was five thirty in the morning. I drove past the visitor parking lot until I came to the half-empty employee parking lot nestled next to the administration building. Rows of expensive cars—Mercedes, BMWs, Audis—filled the parking spots.

I stepped out of my car and pulled off my civilian jacket. It was March. My stomach was in knots, and the gallon of coffee I had forced down earlier was eating away at the inner lining of my stomach.

The chill of the morning air swept through me. I rubbed my hands together and searched for my black leather gloves. I felt relieved that I had spent the extra money on a good jacket with added insulation.

I noticed Officer Richard Chung emerge from a dark corner. I knew Chung from the prison academy. Just twenty-one, with an arrest record for street racing, he had delivered pizza before joining.

He looked tired, but I envied him for already having worked a full shift inside the walls of the prison. I flashed him a nervous smile.

"How'd your first shift go?"

"Totally boring, man," he said yawning. "I sat up in the gym gun spot all night and tried to stay awake. It was really hot up there and it stinks really bad."

I was jealous that he'd been in a gun spot, high above the prison's problems and troubles. He had a full eight hours' prison knowledge on me.

"Did you shoot anyone?"

"You fucking kidding? I almost shot myself trying not to nod off. I'm going home to sleep," he said with a wave.

I made my way to the pedestrian gate and showed my identification to Officer Marcus Wooden, a gray-bearded, fifty-five-year-old who looked to be more than 400 pounds. The officers had nicknamed him "Kool-Aid" because he looked like the big red talking pitcher of Kool-Aid from the TV commercials. Officer Wooden was so big that other officers had a death pool on him. He'd already had two heart attacks; he carried a small oxygen tank with him wherever he went. How they kept him on the job I had no idea. He arrived early for each shift knowing that it would take him more than an hour to walk to his post. He had to stop and rest every twenty yards. Most days the prison ambulance would drive him down the quarter-mile track to the prison yards. They didn't make a utility belt in his size, so he had to use a bungee cord to tie off the ends.

"I gotta search the contents of your bag!" he shouted.

"What for?" I asked, pushing my blue Igloo lunch bag toward him.

Panting, he reached across the counter and grabbed my arm. "Contraband."

I was insulted. It was my first damn day at work. "I don't have any contraband."

"Didn't you get the memo, man? We gotta search everyone." He searched the contents eagerly, like he was looking for a snack. "You sure have a lot of cheese," he said.

I knew officers did not get lunch breaks; I had brought string cheese to snack on.

"What are you going to do, feed the rats?" He gave a self-satisfied laugh at his little joke, tugging at his graying beard. New officers were searched more closely than the veterans, who were usually just waved through. Officers were more suspicious of a new face, thinking it might be someone from Internal Affairs working undercover.

I checked the movement sheet behind its glass case to see where my job assignment was. There were no roll calls or formal introductions before each shift.

Information was passed along in monthly training classes, memos, or by word of mouth.

The movement sheet for officers listed a variety of weekly jobs and vacations, as well as transfers, days off, sick days, suspensions, terminations, and deaths. The jobs were not spelled out but rather written in numeric code, each number representing a certain yard, shift, and position. Officers rarely knew when fresh recruits were showing up from the academy.

I found my last name on the board, followed by "C-Voc." I copied it down on the small pad of paper I carried in my shirt pocket.

"What are you writing down?" asked Officer Wooden.

"My assignment?"

"You shouldn't write things down around here," he said. "People will think you're a snitch."

"Then how am I supposed to remember things?"

"What, are you retarded?"

"What is C-Voc?"

"You don't know?" he asked.

"No," I said as patiently as I could. "It's my first day."

"Sounds like some yard job. Try Charlie Yard," he said.

"There must be some mistake. I'm supposed to work in a tower."

"Who the hell told you that?"

"The recruiter." The recruiter had said that since I had a college degree, I would always be placed in a tower or gun position.

He chuckled. "Shit, boy, your recruiter lied. You'll be on the ground for the next twenty years. Go out to your left. When you get to Complex Control, ask the first officer you see."

Outside the door of the pedestrian gate I entered another set of gates monitored by a rusty video camera. The tower officer controlled all movement of employees and visitors entering and leaving the prison; the pedestrian gate allowed human traffic to flow safely through the electrified fence that surrounded the prison. It was one of the few places with a video camera.

A gated fence rattled open. I stepped inside the sally port and waited for the gate to close slowly behind me. Rarely were two doors or gates open at the same time, for security reasons. As I inched toward the next gate, I could hear a low hum from the electrified fence. I made sure not to touch anything, fearing the embarrassment of getting fried to death my very first day.

The prison was about the size of four football stadiums. Charlie and Delta yards were to the left of the pedestrian gate, about a quarter-mile down a black concrete roadway. I picked up my pace, eager to find someone who could instruct me on what to do next.

As I walked down the long roadway, a number of first watch officers appeared. Known as the graveyard shift, the first watch was 10:00 p.m. to 6:00 a.m. Most of them ignored me. I envied them. They were on their way home. I didn't know what to expect. The prison was so large that an officer could go his or her whole career and still not see the entire place or meet all the employees.

Complex Control was the entrance point before entering Charlie and Delta yards. I walked down a long hallway with empty inmate visiting rooms on either side until I came to another blue-painted, steel-barred gate and showed my identification again.

Officer Jaime Frias was behind a thick panel of bulletproof glass. Officer Frias was a thirty-year veteran who wore an auburn toupee and hearing aids. He looked old and frail. I handed him my ID through a narrow slot.

"Where do I get my equipment for C-Voc?"

"What?" Frias shouted. I could barely hear him through the glass.

"I said, where do I get my equipment for Charlie-Voc?"

"You don't know?"

"No. That's why I'm asking."

"If you don't know what to do, then get out of the way!" Frias screamed.

I could tell that he was upset.

"I just need to find my post. I'm new."

"It's not here!" he yelled.

"Do you know where?"

"Try Charlie Yard!"

He snorted in disgust and pointed to my right, while taking a slug from a can of diet soda. He punched a button and a heavy blue steel door popped open.

Most of the doors had metal plates on the bottom portion to prevent officers from damaging them with their batons or boots. They required a healthy shove to exit.

I passed a broken soda machine and an old phone booth surrounded by bags of trash, and walked several hundred feet to another fence. Officers were prohibited from using cell phones inside the prison, but most officers brought them in anyway.

I pushed a red button on a small metal box, and the gate whistled a high-pitched tune. I pushed the gate, but it jammed. I gave it a hard kick with my foot; it swung open.

Another officer was coming my way. "Hold the gate, I'm going out," he hollered.

"No problem. Where's Charlie-Voc?"

"Over there," he said.

He pointed to the south end of the yard and slammed the gate shut. I stood for a moment looking where he had pointed, but didn't see anything except a wall with a huge yellow and orange sunset mural. I walked toward it.

The prison yard had five housing units spaced several yards apart in a half circle. Each unit had one hundred double-bunked cells on a two-level tier system. Along the east wall were the program office, canteen, library, education classrooms, chapel, gym, medical office, and chow hall. The center of the yard was a playground, with soccer and baseball fields and basketball, handball, and volleyball courts, as well as a jogging track that ran along the perimeter. Because the inmates had used the weights as weapons in yard fights too many times, the weight pile had been replaced with a low-impact workout area with dip bars and pull-up bars. The yard was the size of a regulation football field, with a fence running down the center. The center fence was there to prevent inmates from overtaking the program office.

I followed the track toward the art mural, looking for some kind of sign to direct me to my new position. The sun was coming up and officers walked the yard in a light, misty fog. I walked beneath the yard gunner, who was perched above the medical window in a concrete shack. The medical window was where inmates received their daily medication during yard time. The officer above leaned out the window with a rifle strapped to his chest and looked down to the chow hall.

I stopped at the program office. An older officer with a scar across his bald head and a pencil-thin mustache looked up from a copy machine. Officer Barry

Schultz had just come back from sick leave after having a tumor removed from his brain.

"Are you new?" Schultz inquired.

"Yes, it's my first day. How's it going?"

"I'm still breathing. Nobody ever shows up early unless they're new. It's always straight up or ten minutes after."

"It's my first day," I repeated.

"Just what we need on this yard, another fish." He rolled his eyes. "Did you get your equipment yet?"

"No. I'm looking for Charlie-Voc?"

"Go get your equipment first. The other officers aren't here yet. You have some time."

"Okay, but where do I go for my equipment?"

"Building One," he said. "I think."

"Thank you."

When I got to Building One I could hear a radio blasting rap music from up in the control booth, but there was no officer in sight.

After pressing the call button for several minutes and banging on the door, I looked up and saw a red-headed officer stick her head out the back window. Her name was Martha Haggerty. The other officers called her "Bird" because she had a long neck like a pelican. She had worked as a stripper before joining the Department of Corrections.

"What do you want?" she yelled down.

"I need to get my equipment."

"Give me four chits." She lowered a bucket. "I'll hand you the equipment through the gun port."

Chits are thin, gold-colored coins printed with officers' last names, used to keep track of the prison equipment. I put four in an old plastic gallon bottle of bleach connected to a frayed rope. "Do you have a radio holder?" I asked.

"No," she said. "You're supposed to buy that yourself. You'll have to put it in your back pocket. Just don't
lose it if you run to an alarm."

She handed me a can of pepper spray, a baton, and
a pair of handcuffs. I hadn't realized that I had to buy
a radio holder, thinking the prison would provide me
with one after I had bought the uniform, boots, utility
belt, baton holder, cuff case, and pepper spray holder. As
I struggled to find a place for my radio, another aging officer with faded shoulder patches stopped me. His name
was Donald Tadlock, and his face was filled with wrin-
kles and liver spots. He took a drag off his cigarette.

"You've got the wrong equipment," said Officer
Tadlock.

"The officer in the tower gave it to me.

"Well, that's mine," Officer Tadlock insisted.

"Do you know where I get Charlie-Voc equipment?"

"You get your stuff from another building."

"Do you know which one?" I asked, quickly handing the equipment over to him.

"I don't know," he shrugged. "Try Three Block."

"Wouldn't it be safer to get our equipment before
entering the yard?"

"Never thought about it," Officer Tadlock said.

"Since officers have to walk across a yard filled
with inmates, what's the logic of only one yard gunner trying to keep track of a dozen officers during shift
change?"

"Hey, I don't make the rules around here. You're
not going to change them, so live with it. There ain't no
logic in prison."

He walked off. I hurried over to Three Block, where,
to my astonishment, the tower officer had my equipment
waiting. I dropped four chits in another plastic bucket.

I shook the can of pepper spray; it was half empty. I would later learn that most of the pepper spray cans were empty because officers liked to spray the pigeons on the prison yard for fun.

The yard gunner announced morning chow and inmates began pouring out of their cellblocks to the dining hall. I hurried over to the chow hall.

"Anything I can do?" I asked Officer Schultz, who was smoking a cigar.

"Yeah, you can pat down the inmates when they come out. Check to see if they're stealing any food. Make sure they walk in a single-file line."

Other officers were already barking orders at the inmates walking inside. "Tuck your shirts in." "Take your hats off before entering the chow hall." "Have your inmate IDs ready."

It was a constant struggle to get the inmates to obey even the simplest rules of the prison. The inmates walked slowly around the concrete track like tattooed zombies, never picking up the pace even when the yard gunner yelled at them over the loudspeaker. Time didn't seem to matter to the inmates, because they didn't have anywhere to go.

"Keep moving on the roadway! Inmates in front of Building Two, keep moving on the roadway! The inmates in front of Building Five are out of bounds!" yelled the yard gunner.

Suddenly the chow hall alarm sounded. It was so loud my heart skipped a beat. The inmates entering the chow hall dropped to the ground like dominoes; inmates were required to get down whenever there was an alarm. I followed several officers inside.

Two black inmates fought each other while other inmates cheered them on. Inmate Foster was fifty-two and serving a fifty-year sentence for armed robbery. He was big and clumsy. Other inmates took advantage of him because he was slow. Inmate Rollins was forty-seven, serving a life sentence for murder. He was small, quick, and enjoyed being the bully on the yard.

The fighting continued despite officers' commands to stop. Foster hit Rollins with a right hook to the jaw and he fell to the floor; blood poured from his mouth. Then Foster jumped on top of Rollins and bit off part of his right ear. Rollins screamed, stopped fighting, and Foster sat up on his chest and spit out the other piece of ear on the floor. The officers piled on the two of them, put them in handcuffs, and escorted them outside.

Officer Schultz ran up and turned off the alarm by inserting a key into a reset box mounted on the wall.

"What was that all about?" I asked Officer Schultz.

"Coffee cake," he said. "They love their fucking coffee cake."

3

PRISON GUARDS

Attention Cadets:
Welcome to the Basic Correctional Officer Academy.
You will be required to wear a cadet uniform during
all phases of training for the duration of your acad-
emy assignment. It will be your responsibility to
maintain your uniform and personal appearance in
accordance with these standards. On the day you re-
port to the academy, you will be required to lease
the cadet uniform.

almost didn't make it to the Department of Corrections Training Academy. The night before I was supposed to leave I went out drinking with some friends. It was happy hour and beers were a dollar. It was a weeknight, and the bar wasn't crowded, so I bought a round of beers for everyone in the bar—about ten people. I walked around and handed out the beers. Everyone took them and thanked me, but one guy became enraged. He had red hair, and he was obviously drunk.

"Who the hell are you?" he demanded.

"I'm the guy that's buying you a free drink."

"You can go fuck yourself!" he yelled.

He grabbed the beer from me and threw it on the floor. The glass shattered. Everyone in the bar turned to us.

"I'll beat your ass," he threatened.

"I doubt that."

I had been training heavily in martial arts for the past few years. The training had given me confidence and the beers had given me courage; I wasn't going to back down.

The bartender hopped over the bar and grabbed the guy, ushering him outside. I turned to the other bar patrons.

"Another round of drinks on me!"

They all cheered. The bartender came over to me.

"Sorry about that guy. He's our town drunk. A real prick."

"No problem. I wasn't worried."

"Just do me a favor and don't go outside. He's waiting for you. He's got a knife. You stay here, and your drinks are on the house."

I couldn't refuse a free night of drinking so I stayed. Last call came around one thirty and Red was still standing outside the window staring me down.

"Just go out the back door," insisted the bartender.

I left out the back with my friends and we walked down the alley to our car. I was completely drunk. We got in the car and drove off. I couldn't help bragging about the death threats.

"I would have kicked that guy's ass."

We were stopped at a red light.

"Now's your chance," said my friend Carl.

Carl pointed to the redhead, standing on the corner with his friends waiting to cross the street. I couldn't back down now. Carl was a tough guy. I didn't want to disappoint him. I opened the car door and jumped out. I ran over to the redhead and punched him in the back of the head. He fell to the ground. I looked at his friends, but they didn't want to fight. I turned back to Carl waiting in the car. The redhead jumped up and threw two punches at my face. I dodged both. He swung two more times, but he was a horrible fighter.

A police car spun around the corner and blasted its siren. The redhead kept swinging and I kept ducking. The redhead couldn't see that two cops were behind him. The cops ran up and grabbed him. He resisted. They slammed him on the hood of their car and put him in handcuffs. He looked up at me.

"What about that guy?" he cried. "He's the one that attacked me!"

I walked away and didn't look back. Three blocks away Carl picked me up and I got in the car.

Before I could leave for the Corrections Academy I had to meet with the state psychologist. So far I had passed all the tests and requirements. The doctor was in his sixties, overweight, with thinning gray hair and bags below his gold-framed glasses.

"I have a few questions about the psych test you took a few months ago."

"Did I fail it that bad?"

I was making a joke, but Doctor Rudin wasn't laughing.

"No, you scored *too* well. Higher than anyone I've ever seen take the test."

"What does 'high' mean?"

"A hundred percent."

I had taken several psych tests in college and while applying for jobs. It was a basic test. Only a complete psychopath could fail it.

"You wrote down you'd rather be a florist than a solider."

"I'd rather be in an air-conditioned shop than a filthy foxhole."

"Have you ever been molested?

"No, sir."

"Did your father ever beat you?"

"No, sir."

"Were you ever in a gang?"

"No, sir."

"How do you know you weren't molested by your father?"

"I think I would know."

The doctor was trying to get under my skin and make me angry. He wanted to get a reaction out of me, and he wasn't getting one.

"Why do you want to be a prison guard?"

"I need a job."

"You come from a well-off family and you went to college. Both your parents went to college. I don't get it. All the other applicants I see are one step away from going to jail themselves. I've never seen anyone with a history like yours who wanted to work in a prison."

I shrugged. I needed a job.

He looked me in the eyes, then signed my form. He handed it across the desk to me. "You won't last five minutes in there."

My assigned date for reporting to the ten-week training course was in the first week of January.

My girlfriend was disappointed I'd be gone for so long. My parents were more embarrassed than disappointed; they'd wanted me to go to law school. I was also going to miss my father's sixtieth birthday. No one could understand what I was doing, or why. While my friends were graduating from law school, medical school, or backpacking around Europe, I was going to school for prison guards.

The question why we'd joined would be asked over and over by instructors during those ten weeks. Most cadets just wanted a career that would pay them a decent, steady paycheck. They had heard that a state job was not only good money, but a job that no one ever lost. Many cadets came from broken homes, barrios, ghettos, and inner cities. They were often the only family member not in jail or prison. They were from the under-class of society, raised on welfare and food stamps. They were seeking a better way of life, and the Department of Corrections was a dream job to them.

The Department of Corrections Training Academy was a former monastery.

I arrived just in time. Cadets were already standing outside the main building by 7:00 a.m.

I got into a long line, trying to catch a glimpse of what was in store for me. A thick fog had set in on the Academy and the ground was still wet from a heavy rain the night before. A bald, muscular sergeant was at the head of the line, shouting out orders as we were processed.

"Stand tall and look like proud cadets," the sergeant yelled. "You are now entering the Department of Corrections!"

The line curved through the two-story main building and then veered off to the right. As the line moved forward I could see drill instructors inside, inspecting the new recruits, barking orders. I tried to hug the empty trophy cases that lined the hallways and not be noticed. This was my first dose of real discipline.

A sergeant named Barry Loman got in the face of cadet Timmy Jacobs, three people ahead of me. Sergeant Loman was in his late fifties and in excellent physical shape. He was often seen in the hallways doing push-ups for fun. Cadet Jacobs was from Florida, sported a mullet, and had a gold hoop in his left ear. He was berated by Sergeant Loman for a good minute.

"Holy fuck, little girl! Why are you wearing jewelry in my Academy? You can't be a cadet. I have nothing but disgust for you. I should scrub the toilets with your face!"

Sergeant Loman turned and shouted to the rest of us shivering in line. "One of the first lessons you will learn is you are no longer individuals! You are a unit and will be held accountable for *everyone's* mistakes, not just your own! If one of you makes a mistake, you will all share in the blame. You are not allowed to voice an opinion. You will follow the rules or suffer the consequences!"

The instructors never said it, but the rules governing us were exactly like the rules enforced against the inmates. We were being shown how inmates were treated and forced to conform in prison. The only difference was that we cadets were getting paid fourteen dollars an hour.

"This is nowhere near as bad as real boot camp," Cadet William Brice whispered behind me. Brice was from Arizona and had been discharged from the Army after losing his index finger in a chainsaw accident.

I could feel my heart rate speed up as Sergeant Loman brushed up from behind me and poked my ear with his finger. I reacted quickly by swatting his finger with my hand. He was not amused.

"Did you not read your instructions on the dress code?" Loman screamed, making me certain I'd go deaf.

"Sir, yes sir!"

"I'm not a sir."

"Yes, sir!"

"You will address me as 'Sergeant'! I earned these stripes. So let me hear you say it. 'Yes, Sergeant.'"

"Yes, sir, Sergeant!"

Sergeant Loman fixed me with a glare. "Don't stand here and spoon-feed me your bullshit! It says business attire, but you are not wearing business attire!"

I could not recall any mention of business attire in the mountain of paperwork that the state had sent me. I was wearing khaki pants and a dark-gray collared polo shirt. I looked more presentable than half the cadets, who wore shorts, tank tops, and flip-flops. I knew any answer I gave would be the wrong one, so I held up a form.

"Sergeant, this cadet wishes to inform you that it clearly states 'work attire' and not 'business attire.'"

Loman snatched the form from me and read it. My comment seemed to satisfy him, and he moved on to the next victim.

After running the gauntlet we turned the corner into the gymnasium and snaked around a row of tables, where we were issued our Academy "textbooks," cheap Xeroxed pages put into a black binder that had the Academy seal on the front.

The male and female cadets were separated and put in different rooms for uniform fittings.

The male cadets were greeted by Sergeant Loman.

"I'm going to need you to strip down to get your measurements. You'll be issued two pairs of green pants, two brown shirts, and one green jacket. We will give you a black mesh hat that has to be worn at all times, except when inside. Fold the hats over once and place them in the back of your pants whenever indoors. If you don't already have boots there is a vendor down the hall next to the plaques of academy alumni. He will be more than willing to sell you an expensive pair of boots. Now strip."

We stripped down to our underwear and stood in awkward silence while we were measured.

Next we were rushed outside and into the canteen barracks, where we had to purchase a plastic flashlight, boot polish, belt, key ring, and toiletries. Cadets had been instructed not to bring cash to the academy, yet there were plenty of things we were required to buy.

Virtually our first day consisted of standing in line and looking straight ahead so that we wouldn't get yelled at by instructors.

I was assigned to a four-man room on the second floor. The room contained two bunk beds, a desk, sink, closet, and four tall lockers. It reminded me of a prison cell, but I knew it was better than the barracks on the first floor that housed sixteen cadets.

The door was ajar and I stepped in to find an Asian man doing push-ups in his underwear. His name was Billy Kang, and he had left Cambodia with his family at the age of five after fleeing the Khmer Rouge. He was twenty-three now and had dreamed of working for the Department of Motor Vehicles; he settled for the Department of Corrections for the time being.

Kang leaped up, clapped his hands together, and shadowboxed around the room for a moment before jumping on his bed.

"I shine boot," Kang said, holding up his boots.

"Good job. Maybe later you can help me out."

"Okay, dude. I shine boot for you, too."

There were more than 400 cadets packed into the auditorium, sitting nervously in rows of folding chairs, waiting for instructions.

Sergeant Loman yelled from the back of the room, "Stand at attention!" Then he strutted to the front of the room.

Only a handful of cadets knew how to stand at attention; the rest were taking orders for the first time.

Sergeant Loman was direct, to the point, and humorless. He was a lifer and loved every minute of it.

"That was sloppy," said Loman. "But we have ten weeks to practice it, so I'm praying by the end of those ten weeks you'll have gotten it right."

Cadets practiced standing at attention until Sergeant Loman was satisfied that we could all perform in perfect unison.

Cadets were called off alphabetically by last name and told to group up by assigned companies in the back of the auditorium. I drew Whiskey Company, along with thirty other cadets. We were given a company commander, Sergeant Dan Court, fifty-seven. Sergeant Court had a handlebar mustache and scruffy blond hair. He had a deep, commanding voice and was a natural leader compared to some of the other academy sergeants. Sergeant Court was well-liked by cadets. He rarely hung out with the other sergeants, preferring to be alone during chow or break time. Most of the other instructors tended to show off or brag about their prison battles, but Sergeant Court was a humble man.

We sat down again, and Sergeant Loman continued to lecture.

"Look to your right, ladies and gentlemen, and then look to your left. One of these cadets sitting beside you may not be here tomorrow."

He shifted his eyes over the crowd.

"You are here to be correctional officers, not prison guards. Prison is not about rehabilitation. It is about housing and feeding inmates. Get this into your heads right now. *You* are correctional officers paid *fifty thousand dollars* a year. This job is all about making money! You will be millionaires at the end of your careers. Count that in your heads, everyone. Fifty thousand dollars a year over twenty years is a million dollars. I am looking at an audience full of millionaires!"

The auditorium erupted into cheers. It felt like we were on a game show. Every time we gathered in the auditorium to listen to a new speaker from the state it seemed like we were listening to a Department of Corrections sales pitch. Cadets were always reminded that we were not "prison guards," even though there was really no difference.

"Let's have another round of applause for the millionaires," said Sergeant Loman.

The crowd of cadets erupted again into thunderous applause.

For most cadets this job was their opportunity to have an identity. To be someone in a position of power, no matter how small. It was a chance to provide for their families with a stable career. To others, from such places as Russia, Italy, Japan, Australia, Germany, Poland, and Mexico, it was the fulfillment of the American dream.

Sergeant Loman continued to play to the crowd like he was selling timeshares.

"If this job is not what you are looking for, or if you feel you are not meant to work for the Department of Corrections, the exit is to your left," said Loman. "All I ask is that you please tell someone before making that decision and leaving. Don't just get up in the middle of the night and take off. Let us know, because we are responsible for your safety."

Next, Whiskey Company shuffled into a classroom to get to know one another better. We were told to pick a Cadet Commander and everyone agreed on Cadet Mike Holmes, because he had been a career sergeant in the Air Force for twenty years. Holmes was short, with a gray mustache and flattop. He was a chain smoker and always held the other cadets back during morning runs on the track. Holmes really wasn't much of a leader; he chose to write notes to other cadets and leave them on their desks instead of giving them verbal directions. He hated confrontation.

I had two more roommates. Cadet Aaron Lars was twenty-three, from Fresno, California. He had been unemployed and in and out of gangs for most of his youth; now the state was paying to have his gang tattoos removed. He had a child on the way with his girlfriend, and wanted to support his family. His uncle and brother were both correctional officers.

My third roommate, Cadet Frank Duncan, was a born-again Christian with a father serving time in prison for heroin possession. Duncan was twenty-one years old and had worked in a steel mill before joining the Department of Corrections. He had spent seven months in youth authority at age sixteen for assaulting a police officer. Several cadets had spent time in youth authority and juvenile hall; their records had been expunged when they turned eighteen. Duncan was married, with two small children. He kept to himself, choosing to talk to God instead of other cadets, but he liked to preach the bible to anyone who would listen and regularly held bible readings in the quad area. Duncan did not refrain from telling several cadets that they were going to hell.

Several cadets had washed out four or five times but still wanted to be prison guards.

"Washouts are an important part of the Academy," said Sergeant Court. "No one is here to explain the Academy rules, so listen to the washouts for information. They know the important things, like how to make your bunks the right way and fold the corners of the sheets."

"Your nametags should be on the left above your shirt pocket," Cadet Duncan instructed. "The buttons on your shirt have to be in line with the zipper on your pants. This is called the zip line."

Duncan knew the little things. If an instructor saw a cadet out of compliance, the punishment was push-ups. Too many violations, and they were expelled. The Academy wanted us to adapt and overcome the pressures of working in a chaotic environment.

We finished introductions at eleven that night and settled back into our rooms, putting our gear away in our lockers. There was still excitement up and down the halls and on my roommates' faces. They reminded me of the hopeful people who had filed into the exam room for the written entrance test a year earlier.

The next morning came quickly. Cadets were up at 4:00 a.m. to clean our rooms and the bathrooms, and then be in our uniforms for breakfast at six. The mass-produced Academy food known as "chow" was awful, but cadets were warned never to complain about it. Chow had to be eaten in silence. Each morning a different sergeant stood by the door of the chow hall as cadets waited in line for their food trays. The sergeant gave each cadet a spot inspection, making sure that boots were shined, cadets were well-groomed, and shirts were pressed properly.

Some cadets, like me, chose to skip breakfast, in favor of getting more sleep but we also stayed away from the chow hall because inmates were bused in from a nearby prison to prepare the food. There was nothing stopping the inmates from tampering with the food; with only one supervisor for twenty inmates, there was no way to keep an eye on them.

Inmates in yellow jumpsuits were everywhere around the Academy, assigned to various work-furlough jobs like plumbing, electrical, cleaning the bathrooms, and repainting the hallways. Cadets weren't allowed to talk to the inmates or even acknowledge them when we passed them in the hallways. We were being trained to deal with inmates, yet we weren't allowed to interact with them. Cadets didn't view the inmates as a threat at the Academy, because the state allowed the inmates to roam the halls freely. The inmates appeared harmless. Little did cadets know the inmates were constantly breaking into our rooms, cars, and lockers, and stealing anything they could find.

When something was stolen the cadets were punished: the Academy took away our liberty. This was the worst punishment cadets could receive because it meant we were confined to grounds. When we had liberty we had the luxury of leaving every night, so long as we came back by lights-out at 10:00 p.m. It didn't matter who was responsible for losing liberty or why; we all got punished for it. Cadets were constantly losing liberty for being in the possession of cell phones and electronic games.

Physical training started at seven in the morning, with two hours of running on the dirt track and exercise. Some days we had aerobic step classes or calisthenics after lengthy warm-ups and stretches. When it rained, this usually took place in the hallways or in the old chapel, which still had its original stained-glass windows and confession booths. Cadets were constantly marching in cadence.

Academy classes were posted on the information board in the hallway each day. Classes ran all day long, depending on each company's schedule. The day began and ended with homeroom. Each instructor taught a different class to each company.

"If you get tired, stand at the back of the class," said Sergeant Court. "Sleeping is prohibited. Don't fall prey to the sleep monster. If you feel tired, stand at the back of the classroom."

Cadets took classes eight hours a day with few or no breaks. During many of the courses there would be a dozen cadets standing in the back of the room, exhausted.

A few cadets were middle-aged, or out-of-shape couch potatoes; they could hardly keep up with the rest of the group on runs. Others constantly craved smoke breaks, or candy bars from the canteen.

On the second day cadets were given a sack lunch similar to the lunches given to the inmates, prepared by inmates. They contained a green apple, chips, one stale cookie, and a sandwich with rainbow-colored meat. We then shuffled onto an old bus for a ride to Folsom State Prison. It had massive gray walls with high octagonal watch towers. Folsom opened in 1880 and was the first prison in the world to have electrical power. It was constructed to house 1,800 inmates with each inmate having a cell to himself; now the prison held more than 4,000 inmates. Folsom, like the other prisons, had its problems; it's the only prison to have had a warden killed in the line of duty. The prison stopped allowing tourists to visit the prison after the murder, and shut down the inmate souvenir shop, where the inmates had been allowed to sell their artwork.

We were walking into a prison for the first time and it felt like we were about to lose our virginity.

Officer Steve Stiller spoke to us as we were processed through the main entrance. "This prison was structured after a church—that's how the word 'penitentiary' was coined. The idea was that the inmates would pray for forgiveness from God and give penance while they rotted in their cells."

Officer Stiller was tall and gawky, with three years in the department. He didn't look like a prison guard. His black hair was long in the front and almost covered his eyes, but he was clean-shaven and his uniform was neatly pressed. We showed our cadet identification cards to the desk officers and walked through the next security checkpoint at the main entrance. Then we shuffled into the inmate visiting room and sat down.

Each prison visit we were briefed for about a half-hour. Employees from the prison would give their testimonies on why Corrections was such a great job. Each employee had a different sales pitch. They were selling us a product: the prison guard career.

"This is a good job, but more than 3,000 officers are assaulted each year," warned Officer Stiller. "That's an average of nine officers every day. The Department of Corrections has a no-hostage policy. That means we do not bargain for your life."

We had all heard horror stories of officers getting dragged into broom closets and sodomized by inmates, but we never thought it could actually happen. Reality was setting in. Several cadets quit before going inside the prison. They had to wait on the bus and ride back to the Academy with the rest of the cadets after the tour was over.

Officer Stiller continued. "And remember, you might get a jury that feels sorry for the inmates and lets them go. Hell, they might even get some money out of the state after suing you."

Officer Stiller wanted to take us to the old prison chapel first. It stood in the middle of the prison yard. Inside was a giant mural of the *Last Supper* that had been painted by inmates fifty years earlier. It was still used as a church for the inmates.

As we walked, Officer Stiller pointed to the river that ran alongside the prison. "That's where the inmates who helped build the prison broke stones more than a century ago," he said. "Many escape attempts have taken place throughout the years using that river. One inmate even built an air tank out of some rubber hoses and a football. The idea was to pump air into his lungs as he swam underwater, but he drowned when it accidentally sucked all the air *out* from his lungs."

Officer Stiller pointed to more buildings. "That one on the hill is where the inmates make license plates."

Officer Stiller stopped us at the last gate that overlooked the prison yard. Stiller wanted us to walk across the yard, filled with inmates packed together like cattle.

I was third from the last in line, figuring it was a good spot in case we were attacked. The only problem was that Officer Stiller was the sole person with a baton and pepper spray—and he was way at the front of the line. The gun towers were more than a hundred yards away; it seemed impossible that officers could see anything.

Officer Stiller shrugged and turned around to the other cadets. "We're about to enter the prison yard. Be careful."

There was nothing I could do but move forward, for fear of being left behind. I had so much adrenaline pumping through my body that a tiny drop of blood suddenly trickled out my nose.

We reached the yard and walked across the basketball courts. The inmates stopped what they were doing, and then swarmed around us, hurling insults.

"Look at all the scared fish!"

"Are you gonna cry for your mommy?"

Death seemed imminent. I could feel myself about to pass out. I dug my hand in my pocket, grabbed a portion of my right testicle and gave it a hard pinch in the hope the pain might zap me back into reality.

A huge inmate with devil horns tattooed on his forehead and "Kill Whitey" in big black letters on his chest advanced toward me like a wild boar. He loomed over me, only inches away.

Just as I thought he was going to strike me, he laughed.

"Boo," he barked.

Inside the cellblock, the inmates followed suit, making fun of the fish. The tiers were stacked on top of one another five stories high, and the inmates were hanging over the sides, screaming at us and throwing trash. Some of the inmates had mirrors sticking out of their cells to watch us walk down the tiers.

I made sure to keep my eyes straight ahead and not look at any inmates, but it was hard. We were all curious.

"You're all a bunch of pussies!" screamed an inmate.

"Get a real job," other inmates hooted and hollered.

We were taken to the gallows of the old Death Row, which had been converted into a storage room. There were nine windowless cells that all faced a staircase where the inmates had been hanged—93 of them between 1895 and 1937. The cellblock had deteriorated from years of neglect and exposure. It was like we had stepped back in time.

Next we drifted through the original wings of the prison that still housed inmates. There were five housing units, including the original two-tiered structure. Unit One had the most inmates for a five-tiered section: 1,200 inmates.

"When these cells were first built, the inmates were given two buckets to use," Officer Stiller explained. "There was no indoor plumbing. One bucket was for water and the other bucket was the toilet. The inmates had to be careful not to get the buckets confused in the middle of the night."

The cells were windowless, and very difficult to look into to check on the inmates. The cell doors were made from boilerplates and the air holes had not been drilled into the doors until the 1940s. The old gray stone walls were rough and jagged. The ceilings were only seven feet high, making the spaces feel even smaller.

Cadets made sure not to get too close to the cell doors in case an inmate tried to grab us; nevertheless, we were all curious to see how a human being could live in such miserable conditions.

After touring we were marched across the street to New State Prison. The old and new shared the same mailing address. The design for New State was completely different from the old; due to cameras and careful planning, there were no blind spots. The newer prisons were called "180 designs" because the gunner in the control booth had a 180-degree view of the inmates' cells inside the housing unit.

The three housing units were each sealable, and connected to the chow hall; each had its own recreation yard for better observation and control. Each housing unit had two control booth officers, so that one could keep an eye on the outside yard while the other watched the inmates inside the housing unit.

Where Old State had seemed like complete chaos, New State was quiet and orderly; due to the compartmentalization of the housing units, movement of inmates was kept to a minimum. Old State felt like being inside a decaying mansion; New State felt like being inside of a brand new cinder block.

The next day, our ranks thinner, we were taken to a mental facility where Charles Manson had once resided. Manson spent nine years here, until another inmate set him on fire with paint thinner.

The prison ran a program for the blind, creating audio books and transcribing Braille. The inmates also repaired Braille machines and eyeglasses. The facility served as a full-service hospital, where elderly and terminally ill inmates were treated. Heavy medications and shock therapy were also on the bill of fare.

Cadets were split up into groups and taken around to different sections of the facility, just like the day before. The place was filthy. It seemed like no one had bothered to clean for years.

My group was taken to administrative segregation, a.k.a. "The Hole." Down here, the most dangerous inmates were confined to their cells, fed through waist-high slots in the heavy steel doors. This was the prison inside the prison, for the worst of the worst. The inmates looked at us blankly, less curious about us than we were about them.

We were made to wear protective vests, advised not to back up to any of the cells, because inmates might stab one of us with a homemade spear.

"How on earth could they get a spear in here?" Duncan asked our tour guide.

"The inmates have twenty-four hours a day to plan and scheme. They make weapons out of *anything*," he said.

As we walked along, one inmate took the opportunity to entertain us, bobbing back and forth. "Don't feed us," he yelled. "The zookeeper doesn't allow it."

There was an air of depression in The Hole. A ringing silence. Radios and televisions were prohibited. Inmates rarely came out of their cells. Isolation was extreme.

When we finished walking the tier, we were herded to a small office, where we asked questions.

"Why do you allow the inmates to have pornography on the walls?" asked Cadet Duncan. "Isn't that a direct violation of the rules? I know the bible frowns on it."

"You've got to give the inmates something in order to have something to take away," he explained.

Cadet Duncan didn't seem satisfied with the officer's answer, but Duncan had brought up a good question.

There were rules and then there were rules. The longer we were around, the better we would understand.

Next we were taken outside to the Administrative Segregation Yard, where inmates were placed in small chain-linked dog runs for exercise. The cages were ten feet by ten feet. Inmates were caged to protect them from other inmates. Some of the inmates were wearing skateboard helmets.

"What are the helmets for?" Duncan asked.

"To protect the inmates from hurting themselves when they bang their heads on the ground," said our tour guide.

"Why do the inmates bang their heads?" I asked.

He looked at me and shrugged. "It's just what they do."

At the back of the prison, we were taken to a set of trailers and told to search the inmates' living area. This area was outside the main prison walls, Level One. Inmates were considered low risk; they worked on outside work crews and picked up trash in public parks or on highways, sort of a modern-day chain gang without the chains.

As we set about our task, we were all shocked to see what appeared to be a woman inmate walk by. This was strictly a male facility.

"What's a woman doing in here?" asked Duncan.

"Look a little closer," our guide laughed. "Get used to it. Transgender inmates. They're classified as Category J. We call them J-Cats. They wear makeup and tailor their clothing to appear more feminine."

Because Level One inmates were minimum security, they were allowed a certain amount of responsibility, and along with that came more freedom. It was obvious the officers didn't search the minimum yard inmates as frequently as the Level Four inmates inside the prison: a flatbed truck was backed up to the rear of the trailers. Cadets quickly filled it with contraband. These inmates had single beds instead of bunks, and had more space than other inmates living in dorms. Many of the contraband items were pieces of furniture, end tables, or book shelves stolen from the prison administration offices and warehouses.

Other items were brand-new, like nylon folding chairs left behind at the city's baseball fields, or sporting equipment from the public parks. One inmate had several brand-new NFL hats wrapped in plastic bags and stuffed in the back of his locker under a brown leather jacket.

While searching an air vent above a bed I found a flathead screwdriver. Duncan searched under a desk and found a plastic bag of quaaludes.

Next we went to the AIDS ward, which housed all the inmates in advanced stages of the disease.

Flamboyant-looking inmates were hanging over the upper-level tier whistling at us when we arrived. They wore tight cutoff jeans, tight cutoff shirts, and makeup.

"Do you want to fuck me, ho-neeeee?" yelled an inmate from the top tier.

We were led into a cell that looked more like a hospital room, neat and clean. Officer Monsoor pointed to several pieces of hard candy laid out on the inmate's desk.

"This inmate throws a fit if we touch anything in his cell, so we rarely come in here. He's got severe OCD, obsessive-compulsive disorder."

"What do you mean you don't search his house?" asked Lars. "He's still an inmate. Why wouldn't you search it?"

"I mean, we don't come in here at all. He's our resident ding, so we have to walk on eggshells around him. We're careful around all these inmates, because they could go off on us at any moment. An inmate bit my partner last week on the hand while he was serving him breakfast. Now he's waiting to find out if he contracted HIV. You need to be very careful around here."

Just about then, another officer stuck his head in the cell, "Any volunteers to go with me to the Orientation Yard?"

Lars and I jumped at the opportunity to get off the AIDS ward.

We were escorted to the end of a corridor and outside to a fenced-in area between two brick buildings. On the yard were orientation inmates in orange jumpsuits, or "carrot suits," who had not yet been classified for general population. Two officers were barely visible on the yard, swimming in a sea of orange bodies. A few inmates were trying to play basketball, but the yard was so crowded that they kept bumping into one another.

"Can we go out there?" Lars asked.

I thought Lars was insane for volunteering to mingle with unclassified inmates, but he was young and gung ho. Lars had been lifting weights and starving himself since the first Academy day and had dropped twenty pounds. He was ready to rumble.

The inmates were clearly not happy to see us; they had already started yelling insults. I was annoyed that Lars wanted to sacrifice my life for the sake of learning. I wanted to go back to the AIDS ward. I'd intended to stay away from inmates until after our Academy graduation, when we had weapons. However, I couldn't protest; Lars was my roommate and I'd never hear the end of it back at the Academy.

The officer opened the gate. I made a beeline for the yard officers, making sure to stay in visual contact with the yard gunner perched above in his small shack.

The orientation yard was like a housing project, with meshed metal windows dotting the sides of the building. The noise was twice as loud as on other yards. The sounds of the prison bounced off each building. Inmates on the inside of the housing blocks were screaming insults at us, but we couldn't see who they were or what they looked like.

"Fucking pigs, get a real job!"

"Fresh meat! Suck my dick or I'll rape you!" yelled other inmates.

"Friends of yours?" I asked Lars.

"Yeah, all of them. This is fucking great, isn't it?" Lars was serious. He loved every minute of it.

I glanced up at the yard gunner, who was reading a magazine and not paying any attention to us whatsoever. I inched closer to the yard officers, making sure to watch my back. I interrupted them. "Any advice for the new guy?"

"Sure," said one of the officers. "Stay away from the back wall. If the gunner fires the block gun it might ricochet and hit you. It might even take out your teeth." He smiled. Three of his front teeth were missing.

"What do you do when these inmates start fighting?"

"Get the fuck out of the way. Let the gunner handle his business. He's fired that elephant gun five times this week. Head for the gate and pray. That's all you can do."

The 37mm gun did look like an elephant gun. It was black, with an oversized barrel. I turned and looked for the gate but I couldn't see it; there were too many inmates in the way.

Suddenly, the yard alarm sounded, followed by a loud bang. The inmates hit the ground as wood blocks whizzed past overhead. Two black inmates were fighting in the south corner. A round struck one of them in the chest and he fell to the ground in pain. The other inmate laid down and spread his arms out. The officers ran over and dragged the inmates off the yard. Lars and I followed.

"Yard recall!" yelled the yard gunner over the loudspeaker. "Yard recall!"

The inmates sprang up and hustled off the yard and back into the buildings.

"That was awesome," Lars said.

That night, back at the academy, Whiskey Company ended the day going over our experiences with Sergeant Court. Cadet Duncan was full of questions.

"I saw an officer cuss out an inmate," complained Duncan. "I thought we weren't allowed to use profanity."

"Well, I'm not going to say he was right or wrong, because I wasn't there," the sergeant said. "But those things are going to happen, and it's up to you to distance yourself from officers who are disrespectful. Just treat the inmates like you would want to be treated."

"Come on, Sarge," Lars said. "You can't honestly tell me we're never going to be in a position where an inmate pisses us off. You can't expect us to always remain calm, cool, and collected. These inmates aren't honor students."

"My only advice is to lead by example."

"What if he calls me a motherfucker?" asked Lars.

"Are you?" The class laughed. "I mean, does it really matter? The inmates are going to call you everything in the book. Brush it off. You'll be making good money."

The next week we were bused to the prison reception center. Decades earlier it was known as a "gladiator school" because of the numerous fights and murders that had taken place there. It also had a dairy farm that employed 110 inmates. The inmates grew cattle and grain, and supplied milk to the other prisons and state agencies. Just as we arrived, a parolee was being arrested in the parking lot. A woman with a crying baby stood next to a car with a few empty beer cans on its roof.

We had to stay on the bus until the arrest was concluded. Meanwhile the sergeant went to find out what happened. Turns out a woman had come to pick up her husband and had failed to bring his favorite brand of beer, which made him furious. He was being arrested for spousal abuse and escorted back into prison. He had been free for one hour.

Once we got off the bus, we were sent to the main kitchen to search for inmate contraband. This was the first time we actually put our hands on the inmates. The inmates were shocked we had come to pat them down. We didn't discover any weapons, but the inmates had a lot of food hidden in the ceiling rafters and under floor drains.

The veteran officer leading us on this excursion reached behind one of the ovens and pulled out a plastic bottle. "This is pruno," he told us, prison wine.

We gathered around to check out a clear plastic water bottle filled with a murky purple liquid.

"Pruno is fermented from fruit," the officer explained. "The sugar turns to alcohol. Alcohol is colorless, odorless, and tasteless until other ingredients are added. Those other ingredients are what give alcohol its flavor."

It was against prison policy for inmates to take food from the prison kitchen, but they did it daily. During the search I found a sealed plastic bag down a floor drain, filled with steaks marinating in teriyaki sauce. The bag was connected to a thick string tied off on the drain, making it impossible to spot with the drain's cover on.

After we searched the kitchen we went to a warehouse to search for weapons, even though cadets from another company had already searched an hour before. The warehouse was mostly empty except for a few cardboard boxes of inmate jumpsuits stacked on wooden palettes.

"It seems like we were sent here just to waste time rather than be useful," Lars bitched.

Sliding my hand along the edge of a table, I pulled out a thin but heavy piece of spiked metal, a foot long.

"That could be a good bone crusher," the supervisor said.

"Did you put that there for us to find?" I asked, knowing the place had been swept earlier.

"The inmates hide contraband there all the time. It's a favorite spot. We'll never stop the inmates from trying to hide a good piece of steel in this warehouse—that way we can always come here and find it."

"What do I do with it now?" I asked. "Write up a report?"

The officer looked around to see if anyone was listening to us. "Okay, kid, I'll be straight. Me personally, I'd take this home in my bag and throw it away so the inmates can't find it in the trash. You can't pin it on an inmate, so why write up a report? It's a waste of time. That's strictly off the record."

Lars and I ventured out onto the loading docks next to a perimeter fence, searching for anything on the ground that looked like contraband. There was a lot of trash and discarded wood, making it look more like an abandoned factory than a prison. We sat down on some benches until a sergeant spotted us and sent us to search the nearby cellblock.

The tiers were three stories high, with tables on the bottom level for the inmates. The unit looked like it hadn't been cleaned in a hundred years, with layers of dust hanging off the railings like brown icicles. There was no gunner above the cellblocks to open the door or watch over officers. At one end of the prison corridor stood an ancient barred door with a locked gate; the keys to the cellblock wing were kept in a caged office to the right. Another barred door led to the housing unit, giving the officers a safe haven in case the inmates attacked them. Officers were locked inside the unit away from the main hallway and the rest of the prison. If the inmates took over the wing it would take hours before anyone realized the officers were in trouble.

The tier cop looked to be about sixty, with shaggy gray hair and a slight limp.

"What did they send you here for?" he demanded.

"We were sent over to help you search," said Lars.

"Whatever you need us to do," I added.

"You can run the shower program," Grimes said, and handed me a set of keys.

"How do you run showers?"

"The inmates are on lock-down. Some inmate cut off a Mexican's fingers. Drug debts. Just walk around and ask the inmates if they want a shower. The whites are showering next, and then the Mexicans. Shower them with their own race."

I walked the tiers, asking the white inmates if they wanted a shower. The door tags were color-coded by race: the African-Americans had blue tags, Mexicans pink, the whites white, and "Others," such as Asians, were yellow.

Politically correct names for skin color were not used in prison at all, yet everything in prison was about race and segregation.

Lars rounded up the white inmates and I stood at the end of the top tier, holding open a flimsy shower door made of mesh steel. I stood against the railing with the shower gate in front of me, an easy target if an inmate wanted to push me over the side of the tier. It was a thirty-foot drop to the concrete floor below.

The inmates were laughing at me as they passed but there wasn't much I could do. I tried my hardest to show that it didn't faze me. I felt like a substitute teacher.

"Hello, Mr. Fish. How are you?" one inmate taunted.

"Fresh fish in the shower, flopping around!" yelled another.

The inmate showers were in a small tiled room with several showerheads and a wooden bench. Like a high-school locker room. When the last inmate stepped in, I closed the door and clicked the cheap padlock, confining the inmates inside. The inmates had thirty minutes to shower.

While they took their time, I walked laps on the upper tiers. After thirty minutes I went back to the showers. I unlocked the lock and opened the door. There were four inmates masturbating over a fifth, who was on his knees. The kid couldn't have been more than eighteen. The inmates continued on, acting as if I wasn't there. I shut the door and locked it. I gave the inmates ten more minutes and made sure to rattle my keys before returning the next time.

After the whites were locked up, I opened the cell doors for the Mexicans and escorted them to the showers. Then I made my rounds, checking the windows of the empty cells. The windows were old and looked like they belonged in someone's garage: cheap, single-paned glass, and warped from the sun, with brittle and chipped frames. The glass looked easy for an inmate to punch out or to use for a weapon.

As I was checking the windows in the upper-tier cells for damage, an inmate came up behind me. An older Latino who was covered in tattoos, he looked to be in his fifties, with streaks of gray in his handlebar mustache. I was cornered in the back of the cell. Something told me to act angry.

"What are you doing out?" I demanded.

"I was talking to one of my homies."

"Well, get in the shower!" I ordered.

"I don't want a shower. Can I get some soups from the cell over there?"

Inmates were always trading bags of Top Ramen instant noodle soup. The soups were used for currency.

"No. Lock it up."

"But why?" he asked.

"Because I said so!"

He glared at me like a child, then threw up his arms. I was shocked that he'd listened.

After getting our feet wet inside the walls of the prisons, cadets trained for use-of-force techniques at the Academy, wearing state-authorized light-gray sweat suits with green CDC insignias. We learned holds and take-downs to use on inmates. Cadets practiced the different moves with each other, learning wrist locks and pressure points.

Cadets were first given white plastic batons, then we moved to black wooden batons for qualification. The penalty for a cadet dropping a baton was twenty-five push-ups. It was not uncommon for a baton to fall out of its baton ring holder. The baton made a very distinctive sound when it hit the floor, so there was no way to hide your mistake. During baton training the instructor walked around the classroom with a wooden stick, attacking cadets from behind.

One day the instructor snuck up on one of our female classmates, Linda Robles, a mother of four in her late fifties. Robles was a sweet lady, but she was always falling behind in physical fitness. The instructor cracked Robles on the back of the head with a wooden stick and knocked her out.

Another class taught us proper methods for searching inmates. I'll never forget our instructor's first line: "If you want to pass my class, you have to be willing to grab a handful of inmate testicle." Duncan left the class, complaining that his religious beliefs were being violated.

Using proper techniques, the inmate was to be instructed to spread his legs and to hold his arms out, "like Jesus on the cross."

No one wanted to grab the crotch of another cadet, let alone an inmate, but we all did, except the females, who weren't required to participate. Later we'd learn that if an inmate was hiding something in his crotch, it was easier to have him strip out completely and do a visual search.

To qualify with our service weapons, we were given classroom instruction before going out to the firing range. The instructor was a military veteran with a country twang who smoked a pipe and clearly hated the inmates to his very core. In the prison, inmates wore blue and officers wore green. "I only see two colors, blue and green," he'd tell us at least once a class. What he meant was he only saw blue and green when sighting down the barrel of his weapon.

Cadets were shown several videos on different scenarios related to when and when not to fire weapons at inmates. Then we practiced safely loading and unloading the weapons with empty shells.

Because of lawsuits against the state, we were told, use of firearms were strictly controlled. In order to use deadly force, an officer had to see an inmate in possession of a weapon, and in the act of using it."

Officers could use deadly force if an inmate was escaping, we were told.

At one point the instructor became quiet. He looked around the room dramatically, then he challenged us, one by one: "You think you could kill somebody? You think you have the balls to pull the trigger and end a life if you have to?"

The class shouted in unison, "Yes!"

"Can you deal with the consequences?" he continued. "What if you kill your partner by accident? Can you explain to that officer's spouse why you made that mistake? How are you going to live with yourself?"

Cadets had to qualify on the gun range or they were kicked out of the Academy. The Academy didn't have an on-site range, so we were bused out to the State Prison range. It was a well-groomed, clean range with nicely paved shooting lanes.

We were trained to use the Ruger Mini 14 Caliber .223, the Smith & Wesson .38 special revolver with speed loaders, and the Remington 870 pump shotgun. Many cadets, like myself, had never fired a weapon. We were trained to shoot from twenty-five yards, fifty yards, and a hundred yards while standing and kneeling. If a cadet fired on another cadet's target, or a cadet didn't get twenty-five bullet holes in the target, he or she was disqualified. Each cadet had to have a passing score of eighty-eight out of 125, or we were marked F.T.Q., failed to qualify. It seemed easy, but even with perfect vision the hundred-yard marker looked about the size of a nickel. Only one cadet succeeded in shooting a perfect score the first day—a female veteran of the Air Force.

We trained eight hours a day for two weeks. The Academy tried to pass everyone, but there was only so much they could do with some of us. One cadet had lied about his vision; it turned out he was legally blind, even with his glasses.

After completing range, cadets had to complete the chemical agents course. We had heard horror stories about the chemical agents, but the worst part was knowing we were going to get gassed to complete the course. Lars and I watched from our dorm windows as cadets lined up in the parking lot to get blasted in the face with a can of pepper spray. Sergeant Loman had decided to gas Alpha Company to give them a trial run of what to expect. Loman held down a cadet and pepper-sprayed him in the mouth. Lars and I looked at one another and winced as we watched cadets run around the parking lot coughing and crying. Several were over-exposed to the chemicals and needed to be rushed to the hospital. After that, a memo was generated around the Academy forbidding anyone from using chemical agents on grounds.

We were then bused back to the range. We were lectured about chemical agents by an instructor who was so obese we all thought he'd have a heart attack the second the chemicals hit the air. He had beady eyes, and dandruff flakes in his hair the size of confetti. He held a canister of CN gas—phenacyl chloride, commonly known as mace.

He pulled the pin and released the gas while chomping on a thick turkey sandwich, chunks of bacon falling out from between the bread. We were already queasy just watching him eat.

"Gas is good. Gas is your friend," said Sergeant Little, not bothered by the smoke.

Officers used oleoresin capsicum pepper spray, or OC, in the prisons. When OC was sprayed in the eyes or on the skin, it caused severe irritation. Victims would fall to the ground, blind with pain. The active ingredient, capsicum, was derived from plants such as chili peppers.

Whiskey Company stood on the fifty-yard mark waiting to be gassed. The exercise was to teach cadets to function when chemical agents were used; mainly, that meant not to panic during a prison riot. The Department of Corrections wanted officers to use pepper spray first in a prison disturbance rather than their batons.

Cadets were shown various canisters, such as the Triple Chaser and CN grenades, and how to determine which contained what chemicals. There were many ways for the chemical agents to be dispersed, and many different types of canisters. Most were the size of a soda can. They had pins like a grenade; when pulled they burst into flames and then emitted white smoke.

Half of the devices weren't used inside the prisons because the cost had not been figured into the budget and the state had not authorized their use; but that never stopped private companies from donating samples.

Chemical agents were an officer's first line of defense inside the prison. Pepper spray was deployed often to break up fights, and quell even the smallest disturbances. In the early days, inmates were shot simply for having fistfights on the yard; now they were pepper-sprayed to save the state from lawsuits.

"The inmates study everything we do," the instructor told us. Inmates know which chemical agents are hot to the touch. They place trashcans over the chemical agents, or make their own gas masks."

After the demonstration, cadets stood in three single-file lines, shoulder to shoulder, praying the wind would kick some of the gas away from our direction. We were instructed not to move until we heard the sound of a whistle from one of the instructors.

"If any of you run before the whistle sounds, you all have to come back and do it again until we get it right. My final advice is do not hold your breath," the sergeant said. "It will only make it worse."

Before I knew it, there was so much smoke surrounding us that I couldn't see the cadets standing directly in front of me. The gas hit my eyes with a sharp, instant pain, like a kick to the groin. I squeezed my eyes shut and prayed for it to pass. Unfortunately, I'd never been able to hold my breath for more than ten seconds and I took a tiny gulp of air. My throat burned. The gas seeped immediately into my lungs making them itch.

The whistle finally sounded and I took a step forward, right into Duncan, who was gasping for air. I was completely blind. I didn't want to push him out of the way, so I waited and staggered toward the voices of the instructors.

Apple Company cadets laughed from the sidelines. They were next, but every cadet who waited to be gassed never thought it would be as bad as it was. It was humiliating, being laughed at. I stumbled around blindly until I heard a familiar voice.

"Walk toward me," said the sergeant. Keep walking and let the wind take care of it. Don't rub your eyes!"

My eyes felt raw, so it was natural to want to rub them. The problem was that rubbing them pressed the chemical particles into the skin where they felt like tiny snowflakes with jagged tips.

The only way to rid yourself of the chemicals was to wait. After about five minutes my eyes didn't feel so tight, and I slowly opened them to see where I was.

I had drifted in the opposite direction from the other cadets, who were scattered around the range. Lars had bragged the night before that he ate CN gas for breakfast. He was laid out on the ground, clutching his throat in agony.

The fat sergeant waddled over to him, bent over, and screamed. "It hurts, don't it! You pussy! It's supposed to hurt! Open your eyes, you weak-ass bitch!"

Fifteen minutes later, the effects were almost gone.

"Okay, line up again for round two!" yelled the sergeant.

Next up was tear gas.

The tear gas felt ten times worse than the CN gas. It filled my lungs instantly, like swallowing fire. There was an almost fruity smell to the gas as it burned my sinuses.

The cadets let out a moan. We had been training for twelve hours straight.

The Academy was given a riot video to show cadets even before it was released to the media. No cadet had ever seen a prison riot, and the video was chilling in depicting the brutality of the prison inmates.

Watching the video made some cadets panic, and several dropped out of the Academy that night.

The state had paid for our training, but they expected cadets to foot the bill for uniforms. Most cadets were broke and used credit to pay for their uniforms. A cadet could not graduate without being fitted for and purchasing uniforms from an authorized dealer. The price for two uniforms was $700. Most officers would never even wear the uniforms we were required to buy. They were known as the class uniform, a tan shirt and green polyester pants. Class uniforms were for inspections and formal events in public; on the job, officers were allowed to wear green jumpsuits, which were far more comfortable.

On the last day of class we were advised to be careful and not get into trouble that night. In our last homeroom, Sergeant Court went over the final details before graduation.

"Be correctional officers tonight, not prison guards," warned our sergeant. "You are guaranteed to graduate if you don't fuck up."

The moment homeroom was adjourned, hundreds of cadets headed off for a long night of partying. Several cadets from Apple Company got drunk and were caught urinating in the Academy hallways at four in the morning. They were expelled.

I was surprised by the number of people entering the auditorium so early in the morning. Most of them looked like inmates or parolees. Cadets in my company were curious that I didn't have any family or friends at the graduation. No one I knew felt graduation from prison-guard school was an accomplishment. However, I could not help feeling some pride for completing the Academy.

4

I ONLY WANT WHAT I GOT COMING

Attention Staff:
All employees must report any violations of sexual harassment. In the old policy, all employees were strongly encouraged to report violations. It is now a requirement that you report any violations. Some conduct may not violate the law, but will violate the policy.

By 6:30 a.m. that Monday, my coworkers started to show up for work. I followed Officer Owen through a door and watched him set his things on a Formica counter.

"I heard there was a fight in the chow hall. What happened?"

"They were fighting over food."

"Figures. So, how did you get this position?" asked Officer Owen.

"It was assigned."

"Your position has weekends off and holidays, and they give it to a fish?"

"I guess so."

Officer Owen drank a gallon of coffee daily from a forty-four-ounce mug that he never washed, and he had the brown, stained teeth to prove it. He wore a dingy old cap and spoke with a Southern accent. He had retired from the military after twenty years, and was getting ready to retire from the prison in a few months.

"This is a good job," he said. "People have no work ethic anymore. In the Army, I did everything without anyone having to tell me what to do. If the floors needed to be mopped, I'd just pick up a mop and get the job done."

Officer Tyrone Harvey showed up next. Harvey was a short black man in his late thirties with a square head. He introduced himself to me three times in the span of five minutes as he put away his belongings and packed a small refrigerator with sodas. Harvey had been unemployed before joining.

"I teach self-defense to other officers at the prison," said Harvey, leaning back to place a few drops of saline solution in his eyes. "If an inmate attacks you, just bite him. It works every time."

"I think I can do that."

"How old are you?"

"Twenty-seven."

"Just a kid," said Harvey. "Where are you from?"

"Pasadena."

"Where the hell is that?" he asked.

"Are you serious?"

Officer Goldberg wandered in last, slumping himself in a chair tucked in the corner. Goldberg was in his fifties and sported hair plugs and a Brooklyn accent. He looked more like an overweight accountant with a hangover than a prison guard.

"So, I hear you're a fucking fish," Goldberg smirked.

"You heard right."

"Well, fish, this job is all about making money. I like to smoke expensive cigars and drive expensive cars. What kind of car do you drive?"

"A truck."

"I have a Mercedes. You'll have one too when you get ten years in and a good seniority number. How much money you pull in last year, Harvey?"

"I don't remember," said Harvey, not amused.

The type of vehicle an officer owned was important to other officers. It reminded me of the importance of a skateboard I had in the fifth grade.

"Sure you do. I made 90,000," Goldberg said proudly. "Not a bad chunk of change. Yeah, my brother is a stockbroker and I made more money than he did last year."

Goldberg pulled a small .25 caliber handgun from an ankle holster on his right calf. He held up the gun.

"And if any of these fuckers bother you, just let me know!"

"Man, put that gun away," said Harvey.

"I've got a right to protect myself." Goldberg holstered the gun and then pulled his jacket over his head. "I'm going to take a nap," he said. "Wake me up later."

A lot of officers carried unapproved weapons like knives, guns, and brass knuckles just in case they were taken hostage by the inmates.

"He's by far the laziest officer you'll ever meet," whispered Owen.

I smiled. "Be quiet. You'll wake him."

I seized the moment to ask Harvey some questions. "What's the first thing I need to do when I show up for work?"

"Well, officers are required to sign their post orders. Remember that, because you might get some bitch-ass supervisor that wants to ride you for not following the department's procedures. By signing the post orders, you agree that you understand all the rules and procedures set forth by the state."

"Where are they?"

"We keep the post orders somewhere under that counter." Harvey looked around, then removed a beat-up orange binder with torn pages. I opened it and looked for my position's post orders. They hadn't been signed.

"It doesn't look like many officers agree with it," I said.

"Lead by example. Don't ever follow other officers just because they're doing it wrong. You have to stand out from the others. A lot of these officers are lazy." He pointed to Goldberg, sawing logs.

"What goes on back here in the vocation area?" I asked. "What do the inmates do?"

"They make soap," said Harvey. "The inmates make it, and the prison sells it."

"What do the inmates get out of it?"

"Most inmates make twenty-five cents an hour. The lucky ones earn a dollar an hour, making office furniture, food products, textiles, clothing, and stationery."

Harvey glanced out the window. "Here come the inmates."

"Showtime," said Owen.

Harvey hit a red button under the counter to unlock the door. The inmates shuffled through a metal detector in single file, placing their belongings on the Formica counter. Then they lined up at the counter and showed their prison photo-identification cards. Because the inmates were leaving the main yard and going to another area of the prison, they were required to be strip-searched for contraband. Inmates did this both going to and coming from work.

"The officer you're filling in for is out on extended sick leave because an inmate jumped over the counter last week and broke his jaw," said Harvey.

I was shocked. "Jesus, what the hell did he do that for?"

"Beats me," said Harvey. "He must have looked at the inmate funny or something."

"How many inmates do we process through here?"

"A couple hundred," said Harvey.

Stripping out the inmates was the worst part of the job.

"It's nuts 'n' butts," laughed Owen.

"They should write a rap song about that one," shouted an inmate, pulling off his pants. I watched Harvey, then copied his routine. The inmates handed me their pants, shirts, shoes, socks, glasses, and caps so that I could inspect them. I wore regulation latex gloves, but they wouldn't have done much good if I were stuck with something sharp. The inmates would stand completely naked, facing me, and wait for me to motion to start the strip-out routine.

I fumbled giving the commands. I wanted the search to be over even faster than the inmates did.

"Let me see the palms of your hands and inside your mouth," demanded Harvey. "Move your tongue. Now run your fingers through your hair and behind your ears. Lift up the backs of your feet."

I didn't like the speech, so after I finished with a few inmates I just nodded to lead the others through the procedure. I tried not to make eye contact with them as they were processed; their hollow stares made me feel more naked than they were.

"Bend over and squat," demanded Harvey. "Cough three times. Make sure no junk falls out of the trunk."

It was the most awkward situation I'd ever been in, next to showering after soccer practice in the high school gym. It was a sight that I knew would take years to get out of my head.

"Doesn't this bother you?" I asked Harvey.

"You get used to it, I guess. Hell, there was an inmate up north who shoved a bottle of ketchup up his ass."

It was hard not to feel sorry for the inmates. Being in prison was bad enough, but having to get naked in front of other men was the worst humiliation. To the inmates, though, it was routine.

"Most contraband isn't even metal," said Harvey. "And no one wants to reach up an inmate's ass to search for it. Officers around here feel that only the doctors get paid enough money to do a full body-cavity search."

I wanted to vomit every time the inmates dropped their pants. The smell was so strong it felt like a punch to the face. Every five minutes Harvey would spray down the room with lemon air freshener. It didn't help.

"It's a good thing we're behind this counter," laughed Harvey. "You might get an inmate that spits something out his ass. Of course, you always hear it before you see it."

"I figure if the inmates go through all the trouble and pain to shove something up their ass, then I don't want to know anything about it," said Owen. "But you didn't hear that from me.

"Not a word."

Officer Harvey enjoyed making comments to the inmates while they were processed through.

"Boy, your dick looks like an elevator button," laughed Harvey.

"You ain't right, Harvey," said an inmate, shaking his head.

Not all the inmates showed up for their work assignments. Some had overslept, or were at the infirmary, or were screwing around on the yard. Other inmates had been sent to The Hole. If an inmate didn't show up for work it was up to the vocational officer to track down the inmate and find out why he was absent.

Attention Staff:
To accommodate the "Freedom Through Music" program on Charlie Yard, please be advised of a rehearsal schedule that includes both Saturdays and Sundays in preparation for an Easter Program. The following inmates will be assigned to pass out instruments to qualified musicians.

After we processed the inmates through, we had more down time. Harvey and Owen played checkers while I walked around to explore. The back area of the prison looked like an abandoned drive-in movie theater, with acres of pavement.

I had a key chain full of keys, but I couldn't figure out what most of them unlocked. I walked around trying several unmarked doors. There was no list to check; the prison didn't want the inmates to find out which number key went to which door.

I stopped to read a memo stapled to a faded bulletin board, dated 1995. It said there were more than 800 keys unaccounted for at the prison, and the administration was looking into fixing the problem. Losing a key was the worst offense an officer could commit, because a locksmith then had to replace every single lock in the institution.

Before starting the job, I'd bought a dog chain from a pet store and attached it to my keys for a lanyard so I wouldn't accidentally lose them. Officers misplaced their keys daily. For all the money the prison spent on keys, no one ever thought to allocate funds for lanyards.

I walked through a maze of classrooms and offices, with a handful of teachers milling around. Teachers who worked behind the wall did so without equipment or uniforms. They wore personal alarms resembling garage door openers or a whistle clipped to their shirt collars, in case of an emergency. These were teachers employed by the state to help the inmates gain an education while inside.

Outside, I spotted an inmate working on a small brick wall next to the drywall shop. I had never actually engaged in conversation with an inmate. I wanted to ask him how he'd ended up in prison.

"Hey, what are you working on?"

"I'm laying brick. It's a good job," he replied, placing a level down on the edge of a corner.

I expected him to be annoyed, talking to me like I was a cop on the streets, but instead he acted like we were neighbors.

"That doesn't sound like much fun."

"It beats the hell out of a lot of other jobs around here," he said.

There was a small section, ten feet by ten feet, marked off for the masonry workers to lay brick, almost like a cement garden. The inmates had laid most of the prison foundation, and were continually put to work around the prison. It was cheap labor.

"Is that what you did out on the streets?"

"Naw, I've been in for ten years. I came straight from jail."

His name was Inmate Casper. He was skinny, with stringy blond hair, and looked more like a surfer than an inmate. His arms were sleeved down with swastika tattoos and lightning bolts.

"Where are you from?"

"Oakland," he said.

"How'd you end up here?"

"I stabbed two guys to death."

"Damn."

He laughed. "It's no fun getting your ass beat all the time. Sometimes you just gotta fight back."

"Yeah, sometimes."

I spotted Officer Goldberg walking toward me, fumbling to light a cigar. He took a few puffs then stomped it out with his boot. He pulled another cigar out of his pocket and stuck it in the side of his mouth, slowly chewing on it like a giant toothpick. I didn't know if I was supposed to be talking to the inmates, so I took a few steps back trying to act like we weren't engaged in conversation. I expected Goldberg to scold me, but he playfully slapped Inmate Casper on the back.

"You're awake," Casper joked. Everyone knew Goldberg slept on the job.

"What's up, kid," said Goldberg. He didn't seem bothered at all by the comment. "Show this young fish cop why they call you Ozzy."

"Okay."

"He's got a tattoo of Ozzy Osbourne on his back. It's huge."

Casper smiled. "It took two months to complete." He pulled up his shirt and displayed the tattoo. It was Ozzy all right, chewing on a bat.

Goldberg stopped smiling and turned to me. "I'm going to need you to count."

"You want me to count?"

"Someone called and said they saw an inmate walking on the side of the road. We have an emergency count."

"Does that happen a lot?"

"Every month," Goldberg said.

"I don't know how to count."

"They didn't teach you that in the Academy?" Goldberg asked.

"Did they teach it to you?" I asked.

"I don't remember. My Academy was twenty years ago."

I couldn't imagine working in a prison for that long. I wasn't sure I'd make it another week.

"Just go over to the shop building and count these inmates off." Goldberg handed me a stack of prison ID cards.

"Just yell them out?"

"Yeah, I'm going to the back to catch a few Zs. One more thing: you should stay away from Harvey. I don't think he likes white people."

"I find that hard to believe," I said.

"Well, just watch out for him. I'm only saying it once to warn you."

I went over to the drywall shop and called out all the inmates' names on the cards Goldberg had given me. The inmates responded with the last two numbers of their assigned prison number. Each inmate carried a green identification card that had the inmate's name and prison number on it. The inmates were required to carry it and surrender it whenever an officer asked for it.

"Jones!" I yelled out.

"Here, P-15!" answered Inmate Jones.

I counted fifteen inmate cards and walked back to the office to write out the count slip. It had seemed easy, and I was pleasantly surprised when the inmates stopped what they were doing to let me count them. The only problem was that one of the inmates had been in the bathroom and I failed to count him; and, coincidentally, Goldberg had forgotten to give me the inmate's identification card. Instead of sixteen inmates, I had counted only fifteen. I wondered if Goldberg had done it on purpose.

"Your count is off by one body! Write a memo to the captain," screamed Sergeant Arnold over the phone.

"A memo?"

"Your mistake threw off the count for the entire yard, dipshit!"

Sergeant Arnold hung up. I turned to Harvey. "He wants a memo?"

"Don't worry," said Harvey. "Every time an officer screws up the count, a memo has to be written to the captain explaining your failure to perform your duties."

"But this isn't even my job to count."

"Welcome to prison," said Harvey.

I was pissed at Goldberg, but contained my anger. I knew that I wouldn't get anywhere my first day making enemies.

The inmate that I had missed was furious. His name was Jackson, a black inmate the size of a refrigerator. Jackson was doing life for a triple murder. Because I hadn't counted him, the inmate needed to go back to his housing unit to be counted in his cell. He would miss a day of work and not get paid. It had been his responsibility to make sure he made the count, but I was blamed.

"It's the officer's job to know where the inmates are at all times, because that's what officers get paid to do," said Harvey.

"You're nothing but a straight fish!" yelled Inmate Jackson, quickly taking off his clothes. He was so upset I thought he was going to attack me.

"Like I said, I'm sorry," I insisted.

"If you were sorry, you wouldn't have done it. Don't say you're sorry if you don't mean it!"

"It was my fault," I said. "So all I can do is apologize."

"Whatever, you fucking white bitch!"

Harvey stepped in to calm the inmate down. "Take it easy, Jackson."

"I don't want to take it easy!"

Harvey's voice sharpened. "You're about two seconds away from losing your job and going to The Hole."

The inmate stormed off. "Like I give a fuck. I got life, bitch!"

Goldberg walked in and sat down. Harvey stared at him lounging in the corner. "Why'd you have the fish count? You know it's your job."

"It's no big deal," muttered Goldberg.

"It is a big deal because it's his first day and he fucked up the count," said Harvey.

"He's got to learn somehow," insisted Goldberg.

"He's supposed to learn from you, not from your mistakes. You're a veteran and you're setting a bad example."

"I retire in five years and I don't give a shit," said Goldberg.

I could feel the tension between the two that I hadn't picked up on before.

Ben Cameron, the yard sergeant, came in a few minutes later for what I thought was my first ass-chewing, but he didn't seem too interested in my errors. He didn't even know I was new until Harvey told him. Cameron, a Virginian, had been in for six years, after four years in the Army. He was twice divorced and lived two hours away.

"It's his first day, Sarge," said Harvey.

"Nice to meet you," I said, extending my hand. I flashed a nervous smile.

"I still remember my first day," said Cameron. "I went to the bathroom and locked my keys in there. Worst day ever. So, are you scared?"

"Of course."

"Well, then, you'll do just fine here," said Cameron. "If you had said no, I would have known you were full of shit. It's normal to be scared. If you're not, something is really wrong with you."

He turned to Harvey. "I came here to tell you a pair of scissors is missing from one of the inmate classrooms. I need you to go search. See if we can find them before I have to notify the yard captain."

"Who lost them?" asked Harvey.

"A teacher. He waited two weeks to tell us."

Everything in prison followed a chain of command. The administration needed to be notified immediately when equipment was lost.

"The problem with free staff is they ignore the fact that they're working around inmates," said Harvey.

Sergeant Cameron left and Harvey and I went to the education classrooms. They looked like junior high classrooms, with posters of all the American presidents above a black chalkboard.

"Where do you think they are?"

"Those scissors are long gone," said Harvey. "We'll find them in someone's back in two years, just like that buck knife the plumber lost awhile ago."

When a weapon was lost, the inmates waited years to use it, knowing it would have been forgotten.

At noon Sergeant Cameron called a meeting in the chapel. Meetings took place once a week in the chapel to pass along information. Harvey and I walked past Goldberg, who was still sleeping.

"Should we wake him up?"

"Nah, let the fat fuck sleep," said Harvey.

The chapel was inside the program office. There was an altar and four rows of wooden pews. A priest came inside the prison and held Sunday mass. The state made a huge deal about separation of church and state, but when it came to prisons, religion was encouraged.

Before I even sat down, a short blond officer named Roy Gibbs brushed by me and sneered. "Heard you fucked up the count, fish. What an idiot."

At first glance Gibbs looked young, but then I saw his skin was leathery. Gibbs looked malnourished. Several months earlier he had been arrested for stealing women's underwear in his prison uniform, but the cameras were not working that day and he was able to beat the case.

"It happens," I said.

"Only to retards like you," Gibbs scoffed.

"You've done the same thing a million times, Gibbs," said Harvey.

"Fuck you, Harvey," Gibbs said. "Fuck you."

I took a seat in the back of the chapel next to Harvey. A lieutenant named Linda Linden sat in a chair

behind them, like she was a queen ruling over her sub-
jects. Lieutenant Linden, white and overweight, had
been demoted from captain after her arrest for assaulting a cashier. She was upset that the cashier refused to
give her a peace officer discount. Prison guards always
wanted discounts at stores. Some stores gave peace officer discounts, but they were usually only for police
officers. Linden was slightly cross-eyed and spoke in a
whine. She was hunched over in her chair, tugging on
bleached blond hair that looked like it had been run
through by a lawn mower.

 Harvey leaned over. "Everyone hates her."

 "She's a real beauty," I whispered back.

 "That's why I married her," Harvey whispered.

 I stared at him. "Are you serious? She's your wife?"

 "Ex-wife," said Harvey. "I was married to that bitch
for five years."

 "I'm sorry. I didn't know."

 "It's okay. You gotta watch who you talk shit about
in this place, because a lot of officers are married to one
another or related."

 Sometimes it took years to realize that officers
were married, because they used different last names
and often barely spoke to each other at work.

 Sergeant Cameron blew his whistle to get everyone's attention and the room fell silent. "Someone lost
a cell phone on the yard today. Whoever owns it might
as well step forward before we call the phone company
and check."

 Officers were forbidden to bring in any type of
electronics, personal weapons, lighters, glass bottles,
newspapers, magazines, or even gum. The list was so long
that the rulebook simply defined "contraband" as any
item deemed "unacceptable" by the prison. I saw several

of those rules violated my very first day. Because most officers smoked, they had lighters; and many of those who had quit smoking chewed gum, which could be used to mold keys or block keyholes. Officers were not allowed to read on state time, but newspapers and magazines filled the wastebaskets. And the trash cans overflowed with discarded glass soda bottles, which could be broken to make sharp weapons.

The meeting ended, and we headed outside. Sergeant Cameron stopped Harvey and me as we walked back to our post. "Just to let you know, they walked off Goldberg."

When an officer was "walked off" it meant the security squad came and escorted him or her off prison grounds. It was the same as being fired. The prison wanted the officer off grounds as soon as possible. The security squad was the prison's secret police.

"What for?" asked Harvey.

"He was bringing in heroin."

"Figures," said Harvey.

"He threatened suicide, so I'm gonna need one of you to go to his home and watch him."

"Excuse me, sir," I said. "If we go to Goldberg's house and he's suicidal, isn't that putting *our* lives in jeopardy? And if he got fired, then he doesn't work for the prison anymore. We don't need to watch him."

"Yeah, his wife can call 911," added Harvey.

"Look at the big brain on the new guy," said Sergeant Cameron. "I think we just might keep you around."

At the end of my first shift I went home feeling positive that I could do the job with ease. I did what a lot of new officers did their first day: I became overly confident. It was a false hope I would remember for years. I had no idea what I was getting myself into.

Attention Staff:
The stress upon corrections staff and their spouses is significant for many reasons. This weekend's Marriage Retreat will allow corrections couples to get away, relax, and focus on themselves. They will return home better equipped to face the challenges of a corrections marriage.

The next day, I was redirected from Charlie Vocation to the yard to help with cell-feeding the inmates. The yard was locked down because of a stabbing. When the yard was on lockdown, inmate movement was controlled, and the inmates ate their meals in their cells.

I sat on a bench in front of the program office and waited for the yard sergeant to give me instructions. Most of the officers were hiding in the inmate library or in other vacant prison yard rooms. It was better to not be seen by supervisors than to sit around doing nothing on the yard.

Cell-feeding started in Building Five. I walked through the rotunda. Officer Jimerson hurried in behind me. The doors of the grill gate closed. Jimerson turned quickly, fumbling for the bathroom key that was so big it looked like it unlocked a barn door. The key was a staple of corrections, a unique key only found in prisons.

"I'd get out of the way if I were you," Jimerson said going inside the bathroom.

"What for?"

Before I could say another word the gun port from above opened and a bucket of water came crashing down on my head like a tidal wave. My uniform was drenched.

"What the fuck!" I yelled.

"Get the fuck out of the way, fish!" Officer Rojas hollered from above. Rojas loved to play practical jokes on the other officers.

I looked up. "What was that for?"

"It's Jimerson's last day and we have to get him soaked."

"What for?" I asked, wringing out my pant legs.

"Got you by mistake, dawg," said Rojas. "It's tradition to soak an officer on his last day."

Officer Jimerson opened the bathroom door and peeked out. A thick cloud of marijuana smoke floated above him. Officer Rojas opened the rotunda doors.

"Are you getting stoned in there?'

"No," said Jimerson, looking guilty, and he darted out the back of the housing unit. Jimerson had quit to tour the country with his rock band, the Sweaty Socks.

I dragged my soggy boots across the day room floor; they sloshed, sending an ominous echo around the cellblock.

I sat down on one of the wooden benches in the dayroom with other officers, who were watching cartoons on a television bolted to the wall. They were waiting for the food carts to arrive. When the officers had to serve chow, it meant preparing the food on cardboard trays and taking them to the inmates in their cells.

Several inmates were waving hands made of cardboard out the side of their cell doors, trying to get the officers' attention.

Directly in front of me was an inmate kicking his cell door and yelling for help. The other officers ignored the inmates. Because the officers weren't talking to me, I decided to make myself useful. I went over to see what he wanted.

Inmate Bellows had his mouth pressed against the cell door. His left eye was cocked back trying to get a good look at me. His breath stank.

"I need help!" Bellows yelled.

"What's wrong?"

"Go get me a motherfucking captain, motherfucking right now!" he demanded.

"Sir, calm down. What do you need a captain for?"

"Motherfucker, I don't want to talk to you, bitch-ass fish!"

"Sir, what would you like me to do?"

"I only want what I got coming! Now get me out of this slave box!"

"I only want what I got coming" referred to all the free items inmates were to be provided by the state.

"This is a cell, sir."

"It's a fucking slave box cage, cracker motherfucker! You can't treat me this way. I'm gonna file on you!"

I took his note and walked over to Officer Gibbs sitting on a bench. He glared at me, still pissed, I figured for having gotten the count wrong the day before. Gibbs grabbed the note and read it. He looked up at me while crumpling the note, and then tossed it on the floor.

"What did you do that for?"

"Do what?" Gibbs asked.

"Throw away the letter."

"What letter?"

"That inmate wants to talk to the captain."

"Captain Crunch or Captain Kangaroo?" scoffed Gibbs.

"I believe he's referring to the facility captain."

"Fuck him, he's assed out. He ain't got nothing coming." Both "assed out" and "he ain't got nothing coming" were terms that meant an officer wasn't going to lift a finger for an inmate.

"I don't understand."

"He said fuck the Raiders, so he's not gonna see the captain."

Football was extremely important to officers, and the Raiders were a favorite team.

"But he said it was an emergency."

"Everything is an emergency here for these fuck-heads. Christ, you fucking fish cause trouble."

"I was just trying to help."

"Don't. Don't help. Just go sit down," Gibbs said.

Tower Officer Rojas didn't care about Inmate Bellows banging on the door either. He got on the loud-speaker to taunt him.

"I want the captain," Officer Rojas mimicked.

"You're just a bitch-ass control cop on a bitch-ass yard."

"At least I'm getting paid, bitch," yelled Rojas. "Yeah, prison sucks. Kill yourself! It's not too late!"

I felt embarrassed. I could hear the inmate scream-ing my name repeatedly. He had obviously read it off my nametag when I went to his cell door. The good news was that the housing unit was so hot that my uniform was al-most dried. The housing units had a smell of their own because 200 men were sweating in it. I always washed my uniform when I got home because the "prison funk," as the officers called it, clung to it.

The moment the food carts arrived I forgot all about the inmate. I put on a white hairnet and latex gloves like the other officers.

I picked up a ladle to serve food, but Officer Gibbs snatched it out of my hand.

"Hey, that's my ladle!" Gibbs cried. The officers had a pecking order on the steam line.

I walked to the back of the line thinking that I could grab a spot serving the butter and syrup. Officers were serving the inmates pancakes and sausages, a fa-vorite combination for the inmates because it came with butter packets, which the inmates used later for lubrication. Each officer had a metal sheet pan that held four paper trays of food. The food smelled good. I'd always imagined prison food as stale bread dipped in urine.

"What kind of camper do you have?" asked Officer Gibbs, slopping oatmeal on a tray.

"What kind of camper?"

"Yeah. We all have the American Spirit on this yard. You do have a camper, don't you?"

"No."

"Are you getting one?" Gibbs asked.

"Not anytime soon."

"Well, how do you take your kids on vacation?"

"I don't have kids."

"What are you, a gay?" demanded Gibbs.

Officers were always shocked to hear I was twenty-seven years old, single, and had no children.

"No."

"Oh, so you have a boat? What kind of boat? I used to have a ski boat but I had to sell it after I divorced my third wife. That bitch got everything."

The line of officers erupted into laughter. They talked about overtime, and when overtime would pick up, and the cuts the state might make to our pension. Most of it was rumors taken from articles in the local newspapers. There was a running fear that officers would all get state vouchers instead of paychecks—IOUs—and that the prison would shut down from a lack of state funding.

Just as I got comfortable with serving chow, Officer Rick Timmons approached me. Timmons looked like an upside-down bowling pin. He waddled when he walked. Officer Timmons had been in the Navy and lived overseas for a decade. He owned a massage parlor in the Philippines and had married a prostitute, with whom he had two children. His wife had been denied a green card, so Timmons sent her money each month.

"I'm the butter and syrup server," Timmons said.

"Fine, but you've been gone for a half-hour. I was just trying to help."

"Kick rocks," Timmons said.

"'I'm the butter and syrup server,'" I mimicked under my breath as I walked away, shaking my head.

"Don't mind him," said Officer Harvey from behind me. "He was a fetal alcohol baby."

"What does 'kick rocks' mean?"

"It's a nice way of saying 'fuck off' to someone that you don't know and don't want to file on you."

The officers were in no hurry to get the job done. They always started at cell 201 on the top tier and worked their way down to cell 250. No one bothered to keep tabs on where the last officer had left off, so it was common for inmates to get double trays. The inmates could have been fed in half the time if the officers paid attention or actually put someone in charge. The inmates knew it, too, and constantly tried to get extra trays.

"C.O., I didn't get my motherfucking tray!" yelled an inmate.

"C.O., you fucking skipped my ass!" yelled another.

"That's crazy, C.O., I haven't eaten in three days!"

"Don't trip, C.O., your wife made me something special like this last night! Then she sucked my dick!"

In every housing unit there were inmates who always got some officer to give them an extra tray just to shut them up. The squeaky wheel got the grease.

Cell feeding was interrupted by an alarm in Housing Unit Four.

I set my metal tray down and ran out of the cell-block. By the time I got outside the officers were already heading back into the building.

"Fucking false alarm," said Harvey.

There were a lot of false alarms, but the officers always had to run to them, just in case. Sometimes the alarm could be heard, but not seen. Sometimes you could hear the echo of an alarm from another yard and mistake it for your own yard. Officers also liked to hit their alarms for fun when they were bored, and make bets on who would respond to the building first.

I followed Harvey back inside and picked up my serving tray while the other officers shuffled back into the building. Inmates screamed in fury that we had abandoned their meals without covering them first.

"My food better not be cold, punk-ass bitches!" screamed an inmate.

"That shit be unsanitary, bitches!" yelled another inmate.

"You've contaminated the food! You're poisoning us!"

"Fuck that shit and send it back, pigs!"

Breakfast was delayed even longer when it was discovered we were out of pancakes; more had to be made. No one seemed to care that Officer Timmons had stolen a pan of pancakes for himself. Officers stole food constantly. All the other officers quickly sat back down on the benches.

We didn't finish cell feeding for three hours because of the constant interruptions. Officer Jay Ortiz was a body builder and had to take a twenty-minute break so he could drink a protein shake and eat a meal. Instead of the other officers picking up the slack, they all sat down again for a break.

When we had finished cell-feeding, the officers gathered around the food carts on the outside of the housing unit, looking exhausted.

Any leftover food was a reward for officers' labor, and the extras needed to be consumed immediately. The officers stuffed their faces with leftover pancakes and syrup like they were storing nuts for the winter.

It was against the prison rules for officers to eat state food, but just about everyone did it. Some officers never brought their own meals and lived off of state food, to save money.

"Come get some of this," said Officer Gibbs.

"No, thanks," I said. "I'm not hungry."

He looked shocked. "What do you mean you're not hungry? It's free."

"I don't really eat breakfast."

"But it's free."

The other officers stopped eating and stared at me, like raccoons caught rummaging through a dumpster. I had just set off a warning bell that I might report them. To them I was the food police sent to document the widespread food theft from rogue officers.

"It's not going to kill you," insisted Officer Gibbs.

I felt like Adam being forced to take the forbidden fruit from Eve.

"Just have some," begged Officer Timmons, holding out a piece of bacon.

To appease them I took a handful of hash browns and shoved them in my mouth. The hash browns had no taste. Prison food was mass-produced, to feed 5,000 inmates three times a day.

I learned early on to fight stupidity with stupidity, because it was the only way to keep from going insane. In prison an officer had to choose his battles, because he never knew when he might need another officer to save his life.

"Tasty," I said.

"See, that wasn't so bad," said Gibbs.

"We'll make a prison guard out of you yet," said Timmons.

The yard officers looked pleased and went back to attacking the food carts like jackals on a dead zebra. They didn't even notice that I had tossed the rest of the food in the trash and walked off.

Attention Staff:
Any printer paper containing the text of an inmate's verbal exchange shall be relinquished to the inmate, if requested. Should the inmate not wish to retain the written text, staff shall dispose of the unread text in accordance with institutional policy regarding the disposal of documents.

Sergeant Arnold called over the radio for a volunteer to do an escort, and I radioed back that I would meet him at the program office. During the lockdown all inmates needed to be escorted. A good supervisor would order an officer to do something, while the bad supervisors would ask for volunteers over the radio because they feared conflict with officers. It said a lot about the way a yard was run just by listening to radio traffic.

Sergeant Arnold was in his mid-forties, tall, with a vaguely shaved head. He was impatient and quick to judge. He had been transferred as punishment for impregnating a female inmate.

Sergeant Arnold was standing outside the program office with Inmate Theo Spears, who was black and twenty years old. Spears was from Watts and was serving five years for armed robbery. He still had a bullet in his neck from being shot by police during the robbery.

"Take this inmate to R and R so he can get fingerprinted," said Sergeant Arnold. "He paroles in a few weeks. Make sure he signs all his papers and gets his blood drawn for DNA." "R and R" was Receiving and Release; it was where the inmates came into the prison and left the prison. All inmates were required to be fingerprinted and submit DNA, or they couldn't parole.

"No problem," I said. "But I'm new. I'm just letting you know."

Sergeant Arnold threw up his arms in frustration and jabbed his finger into my chest.

"Are you a correctional officer?" Arnold demanded.

"Yes."

"Do you have a badge?"

"Yes."

"You went to the Academy like everyone else, so handle it. I ain't got time for this shit."

"That's fine, but I'm just letting you know that I don't know what's going on here."

"That's fucking obvious," he sneered.

I motioned the inmate to get up from a bench and we walked to the yard gate.

"When you getting out?"

"Next month, in April," Spears said.

"What are you going to do when you get out?"

"Get a job," he said.

"No, I mean what are you really going to do?"

"Eat pussy," he laughed.

Over time, I noticed that the inmates' answers were always the same. They bragged about going straight or getting a real job when they paroled; this time things would be different; they had learned their lesson and been rehabilitated. The truth was they were scared to leave, because that meant behaving not only responsibly, but independently. Inmates usually came back. They were always happy to see me. Prison was their comfort zone. Everything was done for them.

I also learned never to ask an inmate what he was in prison for. All the inmates believed they were innocent. I had to ask the inmate what he was "accused of," not what crime he was convicted of. Every inmate was innocent and had been set up by the cops.

We walked through the yard gate and over to Complex Control. It was a square room made of cinder blocks, like a bunker with large windows. The door popped open and we walked through. The officer behind the glass screamed something but I couldn't understand him. He popped another door and ran out, grabbing the inmate by the shoulder and slamming him to the floor.

"What are you doing?" he demanded.

"Nothing. He's paroling soon."

"He needs to be in cuffs!"

I hadn't cuffed him because I didn't think he would do anything to screw up his parole. It wasn't uncommon for inmates to screw up their chances to parole by assaulting an officer, just to stay in prison.

The officer was a few inches taller than me, six-foot, five-inches, and thin. His name was Ethan Crocker. He had stringy black hair coated in gel, pimples, and Coke-bottle glasses. He looked like a distorted Clark Kent.

Officer Crocker had failed computer school but set up his own computer business from home. Crocker tried to get other officers to sign up for his computer repair business. Officer Gibbs was his only client.

"Face the wall and don't fucking move," Crocker growled at the inmate.

The inmate didn't flinch. He acted like it was normal for him to get tossed around like a rag doll by an officer. I tried to intervene.

"Easy, man," I said. "He didn't do anything. I'm taking him to get fingerprinted. He didn't attack me or anything."

To take the side of an inmate was just as bad as being an inmate. If you had to question an officer, it was advised you do so behind closed doors and away from inmates.

Crocker turned red with anger. If it hadn't been my first week, I would have known that Crocker was trying to show off. He was a coward when it came to dealing with inmates. Crocker was afraid to work the yards, choosing to stay safely behind a desk or a wall of armored glass.

"What the fuck do you think you're doing?" Crocker demanded.

"Sergeant Arnold ordered me to take the inmate to get fingerprinted," I said. It was always good to throw out a supervisor's name; it gave you credibility.

"You never take an inmate off the yard without cuffs," Crocker said. "And furthermore, you need to present the inmate's identification at the window before entering Complex Control."

"You're the one who opened the door. I thought you knew. I don't know what the procedure is. I'm new."

"That's fucking obvious!" Crocker screamed.

I had expected that the staff passed along information to other officers to ensure that things were done smoothly. But I learned quickly that this never happened; the staff simply never thought to give anyone advance notice on any matter. I had—quite reasonably, I thought—assumed that Sergeant Arnold had called to tell them I was bringing an inmate through.

"I was just doing what I was told to do."

"That doesn't fucking matter," Crocker barked. "Take this inmate back to the yard."

"Okay, but Sergeant Arnold told me to take him to R and R for fingerprinting."

"R and R is closed today. Go back to the fucking yard." Crocker unlocked the handcuffs and we exited Complex Control.

I felt humiliated. Spears looked at me.

"What do you want me to do?"

"Just go back to your cell."

"Keep your head up, man. You're better than these guys."

"Thanks."

Officers rarely took compliments from inmates, but what inmate Spears was saying was that I was building a good reputation for myself. I had remained firm, fair, and consistent. Few officers ever admitted they were wrong, because they could always blame an inmate.

I made my way back to the program office. Sergeant Arnold was standing out in front joking with a handful of officers.

"R and R is closed today, sir."

"Come into my office," said Sergeant Arnold.

I followed him into the office. He closed the door behind me. I thought he was going to apologize for not knowing that R and R was closed.

"I just got a call from Control," Arnold said. "And he told me you were a loud-mouth punk."

"All I said was—"

"I don't want to hear it! I asked you to complete a simple task and now I'm getting phone calls. I don't need to get phone calls from anyone you dumb-ass honky! It makes me look bad."

Sergeant Arnold didn't care what I had to say, so I had nothing to lose by arguing back. I was pissed that I was being hung out to dry just because I was new and Arnold lacked communication skills.

"This is bullshit," I said. "I told you I was new and I didn't know what I was doing. I told you before I left with the inmate. Nobody tells me anything around here, so how the fuck am I supposed to know?"

It was a gamble, yelling at my superior, but it worked. I could see that my words had sunk in, even if he would never admit it.

"Fuck it," Arnold finally said. "Just go help the other officers search Five Block for those goddamn scissors. Can you handle that?"

"Yes, sir."

"And take your goddamn car keys off your utility belt before an inmate snatches them off."

The supervisors always had to have the last word.

"Yes, sir."

The Academy had taught us to keep our personal keys on us at all times, so that the inmates didn't steal them out of our lunch bags. I didn't bother to argue with Sergeant Arnold.

Attention Staff:
The below named inmates are members of the Special Inmate Committee appointed by the warden. This roster will supersede any previous roster. Only the inmates on this roster are to be permitted to perform on the Special Inmate Committee. The committee members will be permitted to access all housing units. This will allow the Special Committee to have an open line of communication with other inmates.

Searching a cellblock sounded like an easy task, but it usually took over an hour to search one cell thoroughly. In theory, cell searching seemed to be the best way to eradicate inmate contraband. In practice, however, cell searches were conducted systematically and the inmates always knew when the officers were coming to search, because getting employees organized took time.

When I got to the unit, I spotted Officer Harvey and stuck close to him. The tiers were strewn with trash and weapons that the inmates had tossed out under the cell doors. Weapons discarded on the dayroom floor couldn't be blamed on specific inmates because there were no video cameras inside the buildings. Several weapons had already been found in the showers or under the dayroom benches, where they could be easily accessed when the inmates were out of their cells. An inmate could not be charged with a weapons violation if he was not in possession of the weapon at the time it was found.

Whenever officers approached a cell, the toilets would be flushed repeatedly, as the inmates disposed of contraband. A strong odor could also be found in the air. It was pruno—prison wine.

"Be careful when touching the cell doors," Harvey warned. "The inmates like to connect wires to the outlets in an attempt to electrocute officers."

"Jesus."

"And be careful when pulling sheets off the ceiling lights. The inmates booby-trap them with razor blades sometimes."

Inmates put sheets over the ceiling lights to cut down on glare. Officers had to strip out the inmates in their cells, then handcuff them through the food ports for escort to the benches on the dayroom floor. The inmates sat together and complained while their cells got tossed.

"What if the inmates don't want to come out of their cells?" I asked Harvey.

"Then they're marked off and an extraction team removes them."

There was a team of five officers dressed in padded black uniforms waiting for the signal to storm into a cell and remove any inmates who refused to comply.

A refusal was an act of bravado, the only means the inmate had to keep his dignity. To the inmates it was the ultimate act of defiance. To officers, it was stupidity, because the inmate was always going to lose. Either way, the inmate was coming out of the cell.

It was astonishing how small the cells were. I couldn't imagine an inmate bigger than myself trying to pace back and forth. The bigger inmates had to turn sideways to make it to the back window; the taller inmates couldn't fit comfortably under the doorframe or on the bunks. Inmate Tom Kramer was seven-foot-five and had used several pieces of cardboard to make an extension of his bunk so that his feet didn't dangle over the side.

The hardest part was imagining the desire to get up in the middle of the night and watch TV, or grab a snack from the refrigerator that wasn't there. Even getting up to use the toilet would be uncomfortable, with your cellmate sleeping right next to it.

The cells were always humid. Even with the door open, I wanted to lie down on the concrete floor to try and catch a cool draft. The vent above the sink actually seemed to be removing the air.

"Do the inmates really bathe in the toilets?"

"Yeah, they call it a 'bird bath.' The toilet is like holy water, but God forbid if anyone spits in the sink."

"What do you mean?"

"You gotta spit in the toilet. The toilet might be used for a shower, but the sink is off limits for spitting because the drains don't catch debris."

Anything taken from the cells by an officer had to be documented, and inmates were given a cell search receipt. This was supposed to please the inmates, giving them proof of which officer had been in their cell and what he had taken. The only problem was that it worked against the officer more times than it helped. When a Hearing Officer read an inmate complaint, he usually sided with the inmate and rewarded him with anything he wanted, because there was no proof that the officer *hadn't* taken the items. Hearing Officers were usually lieutenants, and appointed to review all inmate appeals.

It took several months for an inmate appeal to be heard; over time, officers couldn't even recall which cell they had searched.

Some inmates wanted money, but most inmates usually wanted canteen items. Inmates knew that the prison warehoused certain foods and the administration didn't mind compensating the inmates with, say, extra candy. Leaving a receipt with your actual name on it was only giving the inmate more of a reason to come after you later on and sue you.

"Just make up a name," said Harvey.

"What for?"

"Because the appeals process for the inmates is backed up about six months. There are rooms filled with complaints from inmates hoping to get money out of the state. If they can't find the complaint, it gets tossed out."

When the prison was on lockdown, the state paid civilian auditors to monitor the officers while they did cell searches. It was bad enough that the inmates were screaming at officers demanding to know why we had searched their cells; now we had civilian contractors asking the same questions. Bob Milton was a Sunday school teacher for the Baptist Church. He also was an auditor who took his job too seriously. Bob was in his fifties and wore a short-sleeve white shirt and a tie. He carried a pocket protector and a calculator. He had suffered a stroke; every ten minutes he would drool on his clipboard and wipe his mouth with his sleeve.

"Why did you take that inmate's TV?" asked Bob.

"It needs to be X-rayed for weapons."

"Why did you take that inmate's radio?" asked Bob.

"The name and number on the back are scratched off. It's stolen."

Bob had a list of all the items that the officers could take and everything that was contraband. He only saw things his way.

"Why are you taking that inmate's fan?" Bob asked.

"Because it isn't his," I said. "He took it from Inmate Jones. His name is on the back."

All electronic items had to be marked with an inmate's last name and CDC number.

The cells were filthy. Dust particles floated everywhere and the walls were yellow from decades of tobacco smoke. It was easier to sit on the bunks and look through items when searching, but even the blue state sheets were covered with a layer of dust that I didn't want on my uniform—along with the bed bugs, crabs, or one of 20,000 other prison diseases the medical staff warned officers about.

Most of the inmates were pack rats. They made shelves out of cardboard and stuffed items onto every inch of them. The inmates who had money on their books were easy to spot by their consumption; they were the ones with fifty bottles of shampoo or twenty cans of tobacco. Money was not the main source of currency in prison; the inmates bartered with food or tobacco.

The inmate workers, known as porters, passed out supplies, but they would keep twenty rolls of toilet paper and fifty bars of soap to sell to other inmates along with brooms, mops, and dust pans.

The inmates who worked laundry had twenty shirts neatly pressed and ready to sell to inmates willing to pay for laundry service. Inmates liked their clothes clean and pressed for family visits.

The inmates also liked to keep pets in their cells: spiders, birds, snakes, mice. The prison had a huge infestation of mice. Inmates trained them to deliver messages to other inmates. The inmates would attach strings around their necks so that the mice could run under the cell doors and out onto the tiers. One of the cells had a gopher living inside several clear plastic coffee containers cobbled into a habit trail. Inmate Wilkins found a baby rattlesnake on the yard and brought it back to his cell. It bit him in the groin and he had to be rushed to the hospital. The snake was left inside a coffee can on the desk in his cell; no one wanted to go near it.

A thorough cell search included unscrewing the electric plates and light fixtures to see if any contraband was inside the recesses, and taking the back off a radio or the bottom off a hot pot. Most officers didn't want to go through the hassle, nor did they have the tools.

While searching a cell I pulled a funny-looking object out from under the corner of a bottom bunk; it had been taped over to conceal it.

"That's a weapon," said Harvey.

"Doesn't look like one."

I had been looking for something larger and well-defined, like a butcher's knife. Upon closer inspection it looked like a pen sharpened at the tip, with another piece of metal wedged inside to make a jagged point.

"As long as it gets the job done, it can look like whatever it wants," said Harvey.

"What should I do with it?"

"If I were you, I'd flush it. The inmates in this cell are both serving life, and the District Attorney won't pick the case. The inmates will spend months in the hole taking up space and then get kicked back to this yard. I guarantee it will get thrown out. It's a weak-looking weapon anyways."

Harvey flushed it down the toilet.

Officers' equipment often came up missing during cell searches. Officers would set equipment down on the bunks and then put the inmates back in their cells only to discover later that they had left behind their flash-light, sunglasses, or baton. If it was something personal, like sunglasses, the officers just let the inmates keep them rather than suffer the embarrassment of reporting them missing.

A pair of handcuffs came up missing, but it wasn't reported until the next day. I was sure there was going to be another search of the yard, but there wasn't. The housing units didn't get searched again because the handcuffs weren't considered a major issue. It was too hard to coordinate a massive cell search without more officers, and the prison didn't want to pay the overtime. The truth was that nobody really cared if equipment got lost, because they were more worried about getting the inmates back to a normal program. "Normal program" was when all the inmate activities and classes were up and running. The administration said equipment was important and would threaten to fire officers, but noth-ing ever happened. And officers never admitted their blame because they would be fined a 5 percent pay cut for six months.

Everyone knew Officer Gibbs had lost the handcuffs. I saw the cuffs a few months later at Gibbs' house during an off-duty party, hanging on the refrigerator door handle, like a trophy. Gibbs had been too embarrassed to bring them back to the prison.

When my relief arrived, I stuck my head out of a cell and realized Harvey and I were the only two other officers in the building.

"I'm your relief," said Gibbs, holding a bag full of McDonald's. I looked at my watch and saw it was a half-hour past shift change. Gibbs had left the prison and returned with food.

"You're late."

"Yeah, well, shit happens," Gibbs laughed. "What do you expect? I'm on overtime."

"That seems to be the case around here."

When veterans knew they were relieving a new officer they were usually late, because they knew that a fish cop wouldn't say anything to a supervisor.

I left the housing unit and cut across the yard to the fence closest to the yard gate. There were three officers leaning against a housing unit wall, laughing and eating sunflower seeds. One of the officers was Timmons. I motioned for him to unlock the gate so I could leave the yard, but he ignored me.

"Could you open the gate for me, please?" I called out.

"The Rec officer will be along, dawg. Don't trip," said Timmons. He laughed and spat a mouthful of hulls on the ground. The Recreational Officer's job was to stand by the fence gate and let inmates in and out.

I stood by the gate for ten minutes while the sun beat down on my face. I finally climbed over the fence. While the three officers ignored me, Sergeant Arnold spotted me and ran toward me, waving his arms.

"What the hell are you doing?" Arnold demanded.

"I'm trying to go home."

"You can't jump the fence! That's a direct rules violation. What if the yard gunner thought you were an inmate and shot you?"

"At least I'd get out of here."

"You have to wait for the gate officer. We have rules around here for a reason."

"Tell that to your officers on the yard."

"Did you sign out?"

Sergeant Arnold was obsessed with the sign-in sheet. All officers had to sign in and out before and after each shift to guarantee pay.

Sergeant Arnold yelled at Officer Timmons, "What the hell are you two doing?"

I turned around to Timmons and another officer fighting on the ground. They were fighting over the sunflower seeds. Timmons was on top of his chest punching his face. Sergeant Arnold jumped the fence and ran over to break up the fight. It was not uncommon to see officers fighting on the yard. I hurried out the gate.

I made it through the sally port but was stopped by Lieutenant Gordon Gittens at the pedestrian gate. Gittens was old, pale, and scrawny. His fingers were long and pointed, like stalks of asparagus. He was half blind and the prison didn't want him working around inmates. Gittens was restricted to outside posts, but that never stopped him from harassing staff.

"Hold up there!" demanded Gittens.

"What's wrong?"

"I heard you were giving Sergeant Arnold a hard time. I want you to know right now that he's my road dog. See these mustard stripes on my arm?"

"Does that mean you have more than a year in the department?" I asked innocently.

"Why aren't you wearing black socks?" he demanded. "It's part of the uniform."

"I have on black socks," I said, pulling up my pant legs.

"Those look blue to me," Gittens said.

"No, they're black."

"Well, get darker ones," he said.

"I don't think they sell them, sir, but I'll try to find them."

"Where's your state-issued whistle?" he asked.

"It's in my pocket. I don't want to lose it off duty."

"How come you don't have a nametag?"

"I have a nametag. It's right here on my jumpsuit."

"It's white. The color for all state-issued nametags is yellow. Change it before I see you the next time. You have failed my inspection. Now get out of my face!"

Lieutenant Gittens hated inmates, but most of all he hated new officers. Gittens wore a ribbon on his uniform for heroism: he had been held hostage by inmates during a riot and suffered repeated sexual assault.

That day I learned a valuable lesson. I would have more problems with my co-workers than I would with the inmates. The inmates were expected to act like assholes, but not the officers. It was the uneducated guarding, the *really* uneducated. The officers were supposed to be professionals, but few of them could even spell the word. It was only my second day and I wanted to quit. The inmates complained that officers were no different from inmates, and they were right.

5

THE THORAZINE SHUFFLE

Attention Staff:
Corrections shall provide inmates who are partic-
ipating in a hunger strike with a mental health
assessment regardless of the reason for the hunger
strike. For the purpose of identifying potential mis-
conduct, custody staff shall make a determination
as to the non-medical reason for a hunger strike.

When the prison first opened, several inmates escaped off the yard. The electrified fence had not been operational at the time, and while the yard gunner was talking to another officer on the ground, an inmate had simply turned over a laundry cart and boosted himself over the fence between the housing units.

Later, another inmate threw himself out with the trash. Trash was picked up daily by inmates and thrown into a steel cage that could be opened from the other side of the yard. Because inmates took out the trash, it was not hard for another inmate to be helped into the outgoing trash for pick-up. The garbage truck's compactor had broken most of the bones in the inmate's body before dumping him in a landfill. The prison didn't know there had been an escape until the city dump called and told them to pick up their inmate.

I hit the "Yard" button and waited for the gate to buzz open. There was a small, rusting white metal sign barely hanging onto the gate:

BEWARE: You are entering into an area in which you may be coming into contact with inmates who may have communicable or infectious diseases. You must take appropriate measures to protect yourself from exposure to these infections.

Disease was something that was always in the back of my mind, but no one seemed to talk about it. It was just part of the job.

The inmates were checked yearly for tuberculosis. Attorneys had filed lawsuits to stop inmates from being tested for hepatitis and AIDS, because of privacy issues.

The prison was always trying to save money by banning certain items, like tobacco, because of health costs, but they never thought about HIV/AIDS prevention—this despite the fact most of the inmates were sexually active and many were heavy intravenous drug users.

The gate buzzed and I pushed it open. The sign fell to the ground. I walked over to Building One.

I had been inside housing units before, but not when they were operating during full program. Now the inmates were outside of their cells. I had been able to dodge them for the first week, until I was placed in EOP. It was the Enhanced Outpatient Program building; it housed all the "dings" of the prison—the mental patients. It was considered an easy work position because the inmates were heavily medicated. I didn't care where I worked or what my days off were; all I wanted was the same position five days a week.

The moment I started to learn a position I was moved to another position and had to start all over. Almost nothing I had learned from the previous position applied to the new position. I had to learn everything fresh. No building ever ran the same, and every yard was different.

I walked through the building rotunda and saw two officers in Cell 125 directly in front of me. I approached the officers to ask who I would be relieving.

"I'm working S and E number two today," I said. S and E was short for "search and escort"; "number two" stood for second officer.

"That's me," said Officer Gibbs, glancing through a stack of porn magazines.

"Well, I'm your relief."

"Oh, man, I got a bitchin' relief. Good looking out. Nobody comes this early." "Good looking out" was prison slang for expressing thanks when someone did you a favor.

It was only fifteen minutes until shift change. Gibbs handed over his equipment: baton, pepper spray, and handcuffs. Then he disappeared. The other officer continued to search the cell.

"Hey, I'm Mike," I said, introducing myself.

He responded without lifting his head. "Kinney." Officer Paul Kinney was a tall black man in his early forties who always wore a hat. He was soft-spoken, and had been at the prison for eight years.

"What's going on?" I asked Kinney as he searched a stack of letters.

"Some ding just swallowed a razor," said Kinney, moving on to a pair of dirty sneakers.

"Jesus, what did he do that for?"

"'Cause he's retarded. I don't know, maybe he wanted a vacation at the infirmary."

"Couldn't he die from that?"

"I guess," Kinney shrugged.

"Then what's the point?"

"They aren't trying to die. They're trying to get your pity."

"Well, they've got it. How crazy would someone have to be to swallow a razor?"

"This is the only place they feel safe."

"To me, it isn't so wonderful."

Kinney grinned. "You'll get used to it."

"I'm going to walk the tiers."

"That's a bad idea," said Kinney. "I'd stay off the tiers if I were you. The inmates will suck you in and you'll never get away."

"I'll be fine. No need to worry about me."

"Suit yourself."

Attention Staff:
An inmate was confined to his hospital bed and com-
plained of excruciating pain. The nurse accused him of
wanting pain pills and gave him a hot towel. Such de-
lay caused Inmate Martin to suffer amputation. Effective
immediately, all staff must complete proper inmate re-
straint training.

The Enhanced Outpatient Program was known as the
Ding ward. It was special for one reason: if an inmate
were to get on medication in prison, then the state
would have to support him financially when he paroled.
It was like getting a pension after serving time.

Some of the inmates were there to hide out from
other inmates or the general population due to drug
debts, or for snitching on other inmates. The building
was the perfect place to lay low. It was an acceptable way
for gang members to slip through the cracks without being labeled rats or dropouts.

The doctors got a constant supply of patients to
help them with their research; and everyone else was
getting paid. The officers didn't care, because it was a
relaxed building to work in. The prison had dozens of
mental health programs designed to help reintegrate the
inmates into society. Most doctors were either from the
bottom of the barrel or they were interns trying to reach
the next level of their profession. Other doctors ran private practices, and drew two paychecks at once.

"What is my job in this building?" I asked Kinney.

"Monitor inmates with mental problems," said
Kinney. "Watch to see if they withdraw, seem sad or
agitated, have changes in appetite, suffer loss of sleep,
headaches, stomach aches, lack motivation or enthusi-
asm, show a decline in energy levels, lack concentration,

feel worthless, have thoughts of death, or changes in the normal patterns of performance. Basically, we monitor them."

"You sound like you're reading off a piece of paper."

"I am," Kinney laughed. "It's right behind you on the wall. The administration posts them on every tier so we don't forget what to look for."

Many inmates stood in their cells for hours staring vacantly out the doors and shuffling back and forth. The officers called it the Thorazine shuffle.

As I walked the tiers, I realized that the moment I talked to an inmate his brain switched on and it was time for him to act crazy.

The first inmate I spoke to was Robbins, who smiled with dirty, green teeth. Robbins, white and forty-something, loved ice cream. He also liked to make chess sets out of his feces.

"Need anything?" I asked cheerfully.

"Yes. I want to have a birthday party on the yard with my friends, and I want beers and blankets."

"How about just blankets?"

"No!" Robbins cried. He burst into tears and dove under his blanket on the bottom bunk.

I turned and walked to the next cell, where there was a young Mexican inmate doing jumping jacks. His name was Juan Lopez and he had "FUCK YOU" tattooed on his forehead. I was beginning to understand why officers stayed off the tiers.

"How's it going?"

"What's the frequency, Kenneth?" Lopez yelled.

"I don't know. What is it?"

"Well, you control it."

"I do? How?"

"From this fucking radio!" Lopez screamed.

Lopez turned and kicked his radio off the steel desk next to his bunk. It crashed to the floor and plastic pieces scattered under the bunk. He went back to exercising. I moved on to the next cell.

Next was a chubby black inmate with slightly gray, matted pigtails and two silver-plated front teeth. His name was Kenneth Forbes.

"Everything all right?" I cautiously asked.

Inmate Forbes reached into his toilet and pulled out a piece of shit. He stuck it in his mouth and took a bite. I was shocked.

"It tastes like clay," said Forbes.

"What did you do that for?"

"I want to kill myself," Forbes laughed.

Forbes seemed half asleep and I assumed he was doped up. Without the drugs, most of the inmates became extremely violent and easily agitated.

"What do you want to do that for?" I asked again slowly, like I was talking to a child.

"I got struck out. They gave me my third strike for nothing."

No one told me we were supposed to contact the doctors the moment an inmate said he wanted to kill himself, which was usually what all the inmates told new officers.

"I wouldn't worry about it. The courts will shoot that law down. You'll get out," I assured him.

"I want to go home," Forbes whined, stomping his feet.

"Okay, go home," I said. "You put yourself here, so take yourself out."

"I didn't put myself here! The cops kidnapped me off the streets and threw me in jail for no reason."

"They did?"

"I'm a political prisoner," insisted Forbes.

"From what country?"

"Ingle-hood, bee-otch motherfucker. "

He turned and stood up on the toilet. I saw a sheet connected from his neck to the air vent. Before I could say anything he jumped off the toilet, and landed on his feet.

The noose had been too long. He looked so pitiful that I cracked a nervous smile.

"You thought I was gonna jump, didn't ya, cracker-ass? Call me an ambulance!"

I felt a panic start to set in. I was going to be one of those officers who had an inmate die in front of them. I looked up for the control cop, but the officer was in the bathroom. Then I saw Officer Kinney passing out mail, and called him over to the cell door. Kinney tried to calm down the inmate but it only seemed to irritate him.

"What's wrong?"

"Stop mocking me," Forbes cried.

"Just let me help you," Kinney said.

"I don't need help. I need my MTV!"

Inmate Forbes punched the cell mirror and grabbed his hand in pain when he realized the mirror hadn't broken. Then he picked up his 13-inch TV and slammed it onto the floor. It made a huge thud and broke into a hundred pieces. Forbes fished around on the cell floor for a sharp piece of the TV screen, and ran it over his wrists. Blood dripped from his arm and he dropped the glass shard. The cell door was closed, so we couldn't stop him.

"Shit! Now we have to take this retard down to the infirmary," said Officer Kinney.

"Can't we just beat his ass?" I was so tired of listening to the inmates complain, I just wanted to choke them all.

"Nope, we have to take him to the infirmary. This guy is nuts. He shaved his ass last week and said he loved me."

"Is that a sign of mental illness?"

"If it isn't I don't know what is."

Kinney ordered the cell door open and took the inmate out of his cell to put him in the shower. Officers always put inmates in the shower. They seemed to think the shower was a magical place that could calm down inmates.

The inmate looked different outside of his cell. Most inmates did. The Plexiglas distorted their faces. His hair wasn't gray, but filled with dust and lint. It was hard to see what an inmate really looked like until he came out of his cell.

"We have to strip out his cell," said Kinney. "I'll grab his paperwork and you go bag up his property."

"What do you need his property for?"

"Whenever an inmate tries to kill himself his cell is stripped out, so that he can't hang himself with a sheet or cut himself with a sharp object."

"That makes sense. I'll grab his stuff."

While searching the inmate's cell I found a prison-made tattoo gun built from the motor of a Walkman, with a guitar string for a needle. Tattoo guns were contraband; they spread diseases inside the prison. I found it wrapped in a sock and stuffed inside a coffee can. I set the tattoo gun on the bed and bagged up the rest of the inmate's property. I then put the tattoo gun in a small clear plastic bag so I could marvel at it later. I had never seen one up close and was excited to examine it.

As I lifted up the larger bag it jostled the smaller one, causing the needle of the tattoo gun to prick my hand. In my rush to get things finished I had forgotten to put on latex gloves. The needle had broken the skin.

I ran downstairs to the washroom to clean the wound.

I felt stupid for not being more careful. Avoiding needles and other sharp objects had been drilled into our heads at the Academy. I'd heard that Officer Lars had been stuck with a needle the first day on the job. He was already receiving an AIDS cocktail, because the inmate who owned the needle had tested HIV positive.

Cursing myself, I frantically scrubbed the tiny cut, and prayed it hadn't infected me. I contacted the yard sergeant on the phone.

"Who is this?" Sergeant Arnold demanded.

"I just got stuck with a needle from a tattoo gun."

"Well, that was stupid," said Arnold. "What did you do that for?"

"It was an accident. There was an inmate who wanted to kill himself, and I searched his cell. What should I do?"

"Shit, I don't know. Ask a nurse. How's the inmate doing?"

I didn't have time to dwell upon Sergeant Arnold's lack of compassion. I asked the on-site nurse to look at my wound. She opened the caged door to the nurses' station, a room filled with inmate medications. The room had to be locked, otherwise the inmates would steal the medications. Nurse White was a large woman, with spiked blond hair. She dunked my hand in some alcohol.

"What do I do now?"

"Go to the Central Infirmary so they can give you a drug cocktail. It'll kill anything in your system."

"Shouldn't I call 911?"

"Hold on," said Nurse White, as she studied the plastic bag. "It looks like the needle is still covered with a bit of plastic. You should be safe."

She pulled off a tiny piece of plastic from the tip of the needle. I looked at the bag and sighed with relief. "You're right." I felt resurrected.

When Inmate Forbes learned he was going to the infirmary, he relaxed; we had no problem cuffing him from the shower and escorting him out of the housing unit.

"Why is he so happy to go to the infirmary?" I asked Kinney.

"The inmates consider it a vacation. They're patients in a hospital setting instead of inmates. They get better-looking nurses to jack off to. The rooms are twice as big as normal cells, with real beds. The food is prepared by a chef."

At the infirmary Officer Kinney stripped out the inmate again and put him in the shower while we waited for an infirmary bed to be readied. Forbes was given a pair of blue paper shorts with the drawstrings removed, and no shirt, so he couldn't hang himself. Kinney got a call over the radio.

"I have to go escort another inmate. Just stay here and keep an eye on Forbes. He's now on suicide watch."

"Okay."

"Don't sweat it, dawg. It's easy money."

I roamed the hallways looking into the infirmary beds at the comatose inmates. There were two inmates who were comatose. Inmate Anderson was thirty-two and had suffered a stroke while smoking crack in his cell.

Inmate Craig Masters was fifty-one and had fallen on the prison yard during a basketball game and suffered a brain aneurysm. Because they needed to be watched twenty-four hours a day, they were every officer's overtime dream job.

The infirmary alarm sounded and a blue light flashed wildly down the halls. I looked up and down until I saw a nurse rushing toward the end of the hall where I had left Inmate Forbes. I followed the nurse and found him struggling to get the shower door open. Forbes had taken his paper shorts and hanged himself on the shower door by twisting them into a noose. The door was no more than six feet high, but Forbes had used his body weight as an anchor to try and break his own neck.

The nurse swung the door open and used a pair of scissors to cut off the paper shorts strangling the inmate. I grabbed Forbes and held him up to relieve some of the pressure; he fell to the floor as the nurse checked for a pulse. Forbes' arms were bleeding. He had sliced them on the edge of the shower door.

"Holy shit," I said.

"We need a stretcher!" yelled the nurse "He's not breathing!"

Nurse Tripodi brought a stretcher. Tripodi was from Italy, a heavy-set man in his late fifties with a crooked nose. Nurse Tripodi started CPR on the way to the emergency room. Inmate Forbes was supposed to be shackled down, but the EKG showed that he was flat-lining. The nurse took out the defibrillator paddles and slammed them against the inmate's chest, shouting, "Clear!"

"Nobody dies on my watch!" shouted nurse Tripodi. "I'm hitting him again. Clear!"

"Fuck it, he's dead," said another nurse

"Say hello to Jesus for me," said Nurse Tripodi.

Nurse Tripodi hit Inmate Forbes one more time with the paddles, and his body jerked up like he had just been hit with a bolt of lightning, gasping for breath. The green screen on the machine beeped and jumped a few lines to show that his heart was ticking again.

"I told you he wasn't dead," Tripodi smirked.

The inmate was alive, but not conscious.

Doctor Max stuck his head in the room. "He needs to go to the hospital."

Doctor Max, seventy-five, had a hunchback and was originally from Israel. He owned a private medical practice in South Central Los Angeles and also worked the graveyard shift at the prison.

Paramedics arrived from outside the prison and prepared the inmate to be taken to the hospital. I handcuffed Forbes to the stretcher. A sergeant was supposed to go with us but there weren't any available, so the watch commander made me an acting sergeant.

I sat in the back of the ambulance with the inmate. The prison transported hundreds of inmates to outside hospitals each year for surgeries and medical treatments.

There were two other officers in a broken-down van that followed behind the ambulance in case the inmate tried to escape. A "body receipt" for the inmate was issued to me. This was a form in triplicate that identiied the inmate, like a passport. I briefly read Inmate Forbes' paperwork. He was serving 400 years for forcible rape, robbery, sodomy, and a triple murder.

Inmates were ranked by a points system. Depending on good behavior, they could drop points over time. A Level Four inmate was under a hundred points. Inmate Forbes had 600 points. He was sleeping, but I still didn't feel safe locked in the back of an ambulance with a cold-blooded killer.

The chase car followed us for a few blocks, and then disappeared.

I followed the paramedics into the hospital, making sure that the inmate didn't get out of his leg irons and handcuffs. A nurse stopped me in the hallway.

"You need to take the cuffs off the inmate," she said. "He's a patient now."

I didn't understand how passing through hospital doors suddenly made the inmate a saint, but it did. Hospital staff always viewed the inmates as patients. They also didn't like the officers. Too many officers had been caught sleeping on duty or sexually harassing the female nurses. Officer Dwight Beers had been photographed sleeping by a nurse, who sent the pictures to the media, where they made the front page. Beers was suspended, but didn't get fired. He was finally terminated months later for fondling inmates while they slept after surgery.

"I can't take off the cuffs," I said. "He's a serial killer."

She frowned. "Oh, my. Well, then just leave them on, but make sure they're loose. The handcuffs cut off circulation to the limbs. Last year that Barboza guy ended up with a large settlement from our hospital because the officers forgot to loosen his cuffs."

"I'll make sure he keeps his limbs."

"Thank you," she said.

Inmate Barboza had been taken to this hospital after getting stabbed on the prison yard. He had been expected to make a full recovery from his stab wounds, but officers neglected to loosen his shackles and his right arm had to be amputated after turning gangrenous. He won a million-dollar settlement from the state, then died after drinking a lethal dose of pruno in his prison cell.

The most important thing to watch for in the hospital wasn't the inmate, but the medical staff and hospital employees. It was not uncommon to find hospital workers smuggling in contraband such as fast food or cigarettes for the inmates because they pitied them.

Visitors coming to see inmates needed to be monitored as well.

It didn't seem like a big deal to let family members see the hospitalized inmates, but then I heard about a woman who'd shown up to see her father in the middle of the night. Inmate Pedro Sanchez was about to die. The young woman pleaded with Officer Beers to let her give her father one last kiss on the cheek. Officer Beers felt sorry for her and let her have a moment with her dying father. The woman was in tears as she bent over her father, then she ripped the feeding tube and oxygen cords from him. The inmate died. He had been sent to prison for raping her. She had sworn revenge.

Such incidents were the main reason that the hospitals didn't like taking inmates from the prison, but by law they had to.

I was curious why Inmate Forbes had wanted to kill himself, so after the nurse shot him up with enough dope to stun a rhinoceros, I asked him.

"What'd you do it for?"

"Do what?" Forbes said. He kept his head back on his pillow and his eyes forward, glued to the television.

"You tried to kill yourself."

"I did?"

"Well, why do you think you're here?"

"Shit, I don't know. I just woke up here. That ain't my fault."

"You pretty much died back there. Any reason why?"

"I ain't got no reason to live. Nobody cares about me."

"Really?"

"No, ya crazy-ass trick. I'm just fuckin' with ya. I was just bored. I like the pudding here. Plus, I can jack off to the nurses. I didn't want to see Jesus."

"It sure looked like you did."

"Ain't no thing but a chicken wing," Forbes laughed giddily.

Inmate Forbes seemed like he didn't have a care in the world. When the nurse brought him his dinner he perked up even more. Forbes sat up with a gleaming smile on his silver-plated teeth, salivating over his pudding. It was his tenth suicide attempt that year.

The two chase officers came into the room late, eating cheeseburgers, dripping mayonnaise on their uniforms. One of them was Officer Beers.

The other officer was Victor Chavez, who had worked twenty years for the Post Office. Some officers drew a second pension along with prison pay. They called it double dipping. Veteran officers were notorious for being late, lazy, and overtime-hogs. Officer Chavez, who was in his sixties, was no exception, and was bitter that he hadn't started the prison in his early twenties. Chavez complained constantly. He'd been married five times, and now lived out of an RV that he parked on prison grounds. He made just enough money to pay his ex-wives' alimony. Chavez hated helping out new officers.

"What are you doing here?" Chavez demanded, sucking on a milkshake with difficulty.

"Working."

"What's your job position?"

"New guy."

The department paid out billions of dollars in overtime to officers each year and the budget was always in a deficit. Prison administrators were always trying to come up with creative ways to cut costs, and when they did, the union always sued.

"No, it isn't!" Chavez said, raising his voice. "You're a leech."

"I am?"

"You take our overtime money. It's keeping me from buying my new boat."

"It's not my fault you can't manage your money."

New officers were always blamed for the problems of veteran officers. I couldn't believe I was getting the third degree for doing my job. I felt like I was in a parallel world, where all the officers were lazy, the inmates crazy, and the medical staff was oblivious.

I disliked Chavez so much that I took solace in hearing Inmate Forbes talk shit to the old-timer when he stuck his head in the room.

"You're a bitch," Forbes shouted at Chavez with a laugh. "Shut the fuck up!"

"That's right," said Chavez. "I'm a bitch eight hours a day but you're a bitch twenty-four hours a day. I have a choice to be a bitch or not, but that's all you'll ever be because you're a bitch for life. You get to live, eat, shit, and shower with men."

Forbes smiled. "You just got turned out yesterday, so you's a bitch."

I made the mistake of interrupting their domestic squabble.

"Look, man, you're not going to win this battle. Just go outside and leave the inmate alone."

"Fuck that," said Chavez. "That motherfucker is a punk and I'm not going to listen to a bitch like that."

I felt bad for Forbes and bitterness toward Chavez for stooping to his level.

The watch commander interrupted the screaming match when he called me over the radio to go back and count the building. There had been an escape at the private institution a few miles away, and officers had been sent there to assist.

The private prisons employed private security guards who made lower wages than we did, but still performed the same duties as state officers. Most of the escapes there occurred because they were low-security facilities. Then it was up to the state officers to go find the escaped inmates, who were usually at their mother's house hiding in the attic. Inmates didn't have any other place to go.

I left Inmate Forbes at the hospital, happily eating banana pudding and watching *Saved by the Bell* on the hospital television.

Attention Staff:
The Director has ordered an end to the policy permitting male officers to pat down female inmates. The searches are now deemed sexual abuse of female inmates and will not be tolerated.

When I got back to the building I was surprised to find an older female officer named Tosha Simon sitting in a chair watching television. Officer Simon was well-known for being drunk. She had been on the news in a high-speed police chase with her newborn in the car. Child Services had taken away her kids until she finished her parenting classes and Alcoholics Anonymous.

"What's up?" Simon asked.

"How long have you been here?"

It was almost count time. Officer Simon smelled of alcohol and was slurring her words.

"Oh, about two hours," she yawned.

"Did you count the building yet?"

"Oh no, it's too dark in these cells."

"You could use a flashlight."

"I'm on overtime and I'm a veteran. I shouldn't have to count."

"Why's that?"

She smiled and pointed to the hash marks on her sleeve, letting me know she had more than fifteen years in the department. Count time was in less than five minutes and it didn't appear she was going to get off her ass to do it. The 6:00 p.m. count was easier, because the inmates were supposed to stand up, have their lights on, and be awake. It was called a standing count. The ten o'clock count was more difficult: the inmates were in bed under their covers and the cell lights were out. Officers were required to check to see if the inmates were alive.

"So you're not going to help me count?" I asked.

"Let me let you in on a little secret around here," she said.

"Okay, what?"

"When a male officer is lazy, the other officers complain. When it's a female officer being lazy, it's expected that the men pick up the slack. If a male officer discharges a weapon that almost kills another officer, he's fired. A female in the same situation is rewarded with a better, less stressful position. If a female officer is somewhat decent looking she can get a job ahead of other male officers who have more experience. If she has big tits, then she can get a job at a desk away from inmates and on second watch. If she's fucking a supervisor, then she never has to worry about anything, and she gets weekends off. Every woman around here has been the token whore on a yard. If you ain't fuckin' a supervisor, your ass is getting redirected every day."

"So what's your excuse?"

"I can suck a dick," Simon smiled.

The Academy had failed to teach us the politics of prison. It had also failed to teach us the count process, so cadets never really understood it until we got to our institutions. Each building had to turn in a count slip, then each yard turned in its count slips to Central Control, who sent all the count slips in a package. After an officer counted, he went into the office and sat in front of a brown count phone with no buttons that was connected to Central Control. When the phone rang, the officer sat silently waiting for Central Control to ask the question.

"Bravo One, what's your count?" asked Central Control.

"A positive count of 198 inmates."

"That's a good count."

All prisons had to be cleared before officers could leave the yard and go home. No new officers knew to fill out a count slip or wait in the office for the count phone to ring; they just assumed that the prison knew all the inmates were safe. New officers would walk off the yard to go home and the sergeant in Central Control would order them back to the yard, where all the veteran officers would be standing around laughing at the new guy. It was a hazing ritual for new officers, and veteran officers loved to watch.

After I counted the building I was redirected again to Building Three to help the officers on the floor lock up their building.

When I arrived, the cellblock had already been counted, but the inmates weren't in their cells. There was one female officer on the dayroom floor. Her name was Elaine Gowns but everyone referred to her as Officer "Clowns" because she looked like a clown, with her heavy blue eyeliner, glossy red lipstick, and curly blond wig. Officer Gowns was in her forties, and bragged that she was getting ready to join the Secret Service. Along with too much makeup, she also wore too much equipment: three badges, a cowboy hat, a scarf, black leather gloves, and knee-high leather boots. She was infamous for getting her baton taken from her by inmates—three times. She stood at the podium flashing her flashlight at the inmates, who ignored her.

The sight of another officer seemed to move the inmates along a little quicker. Many officers stood at the podium and shined their flashlights at the inmates. The inmates always ignored the flashlight, like an irritating ray of sunlight streaming through a crack in a bedroom window. The best way, I thought, to get inmates in their cells was to chase them around and pester them until they locked up. It was a tiring process, but effective. I still couldn't believe that the state would approve only two officers to lock up 200 inmates.

While shooing an inmate into his cell on the upper tier, I noticed an officer sitting on the bunk inside a cell watching TV with an inmate. It was Officer Gibbs.

"What are you doing?" Gibbs asked.

"Locking up the unit. What are you doing?"

"I'm doing a cell search," he said with a grin.

"It's past count time."

"Shit. It is?" Gibbs looked at his watch.

"That's why they sent me over. To lock up the building. They said there weren't any officers in this building."

Gibbs stood up and shook the inmate's hand. "I'll catch you later, dawg," he said as he walked out of the cell.

"Aren't you going to help me lock up?"

"Sorry, dawg. This ain't my building. I'm on overtime. I gotta go wait for my relief."

Gibbs hurried down the tier, down the stairs, and out of the building. I continued down the tier, telling inmates to step inside their cells so the control officer could close the cell doors. The inmates stood in front of the cell doors and blocked them with their feet so they could get a few extra seconds to talk to their neighbors.

Another inmate across the tier shouted out to the control officer to open his cell door. To my horror, the female officer in the tower hit the button and opened the cell door without even looking in my direction. She had assumed that I had called out to open the cell door, and was busy talking to someone on the phone. She was so distracted she would never know if an inmate had dragged me in a cell and beaten me unconscious. An easy escape for an inmate would be to take an officer's uniform and walk out of the prison.

"Man, stop fucking around and lock it back up!" I shouted to the inmate.

The last thing I wanted at that point was to have problems, but the inmate stepped out of his cell and came toward me with a sinister smile. I looked around and we were the last two standing on the tier. I glanced at my watch; it was five minutes to ten. I could see officers walking to the yard gate through the windows. I didn't have an alarm to hit, and any cries for help would only make me look weak. I could tell something was wrong with the inmate by the way he staggered out of the cell. He looked drunk. The inmates were full of liquid courage after drinking pruno. The prison forbade inmates from drinking alcohol, yet provided them with all the ingredients to make it.

I checked his door tag. His name was Freddy Davis and he was an old "C" number. He had already been in prison for more than twenty years. He was serving life for the murder of a Sunday school teacher. A prison number started with a letter of the alphabet, followed by five numbers. When the prison system filled in 10,000 prison numbers, then the letter would change to a "B." When I started, the inmates were being assigned the letter "P."

"Do you think you can take me?" Davis demanded.

"Just lock it up, fool."

I knew I could take him, but I also knew I wanted to go home. I didn't feel like writing reports all night. I could have sprayed him with mace and called it a day. The inmates were supposed to have been locked up a half-hour ago. I knew I'd get blamed.

"I think I can beat your fish ass!" Davis yelled. He stopped for a moment and stared me down, waiting for me to run away.

I stood my ground. "Look, man," I said. "We could roll around on the tier for a while until the responding staff gets here. If you kick my ass, that's great. But I guarantee you those ten cops are going to stomp your head. The choice is yours."

"That's some fucked-up shit, C.O.!" said Davis.

"The choice is yours."

"Get your dumb ass back in the house," yelled another inmate from a cell nearby.

To my surprise Davis turned and darted back into his cell. The control cop finally noticed me on the tier and closed the cell door.

I had been at the prison for three weeks.

I was so stressed that day that I decided to quit. I marched over to the watch commander's office intending to turn in my badge, but no one was there. I collected my thoughts and went home.

6
JUST GAY FOR THE STAY

Attention Staff:
In the summer months, particularly July and August, blood donations drop due to college and high school students returning home or on break. These students contribute 33 percent of blood donations each year. Due to the low blood supply, our local American Red Cross will be in the employee parking lot this Friday. We encourage all employees to participate.

The Academy had strongly suggested living more than half an hour from the prison so that officers would have drive time to cool down after work. That way an officer didn't come home and take his anger out on his family. Prison guards had a high rate of spousal abuse and alcoholism.

"Leave it at the gate and don't take it home," stressed Sergeant Court.

I never saw the point, because I lived more than a hundred miles away, in Pasadena. I was putting 60,000 miles a year on my car and it took me an hour and a half to get to work each day. Not to mention gas cost me more than $600 a month. To me, a longer drive just meant I had more time to dwell on my hatred for the inmates and the prison. I wanted to live closer so that I could get home quicker and have time to relax before coming back to work. I didn't think I'd be there for much longer anyway. To save money, I carpooled with a variety of officers, including many I could not stand and stopped carpooling with after a while. A lot of officers drove in a van pool or rented a crash pad and went home on their days off.

One Friday night, after dropping off an officer, I was pulled over by the police. It was about eleven-thirty, and the police ordered me out of my car with my hands up.

"Drop the weapon!" the cops ordered.

All I had in my hand were my car keys. I was standing in the middle of the street with two guns drawn on me in a felony stop.

"I don't have a weapon!"

"Drop what's in your hand!"

I dropped the keys on the ground.

"Now get down on your stomach and spread your legs!"

I got down on my stomach and spread my legs. A male officer pulled my arms behind my back and hand-cuffed me.

"What are you doing in this neighborhood?"

"I just got off work. I was dropping my partner off at home."

"Where does he live?"

"Around the corner."

"What's the name of the street?"

"I don't know the street."

"You were buying drugs, weren't you?"

"No, sir. I just got off work."

"Don't you fucking lie to me."

Even though I wore my uniform, I was being treated like a criminal. I knew the best thing to do was be patient. The cop pulled me up and walked me to the back of the trunk. He pushed me against the patrol car.

"I'm gonna ask you again. What are you doing in this neighborhood?"

"I just got off work. I'm a corrections officer."

He made sure to grab my balls. He pulled out my ID card and read it. The other officer searched my car. He found my utility belt and held it up.

"What the fuck is this?"

"It's my work belt. I work at the prison."

The cops hated prison guards because we obtained better contracts and received better pay raises. The cops would never step inside a prison; still, they had no re-spect for prison guards because we weren't considered "real" peace officers.

The cop found my badge, but still wasn't going to back down.

"You're in a known gang area, so you should watch out driving around here."

I was uncuffed and given my car keys back. I had mixed emotions about being pulled over for no reason. I knew they were just doing their job, and had I been a criminal, they would have taken me off the streets. However, I was disturbed by the way I was treated, even after they found out that I worked at the prison.

On my way in the next day I was stopped by fellow fish Richard Chung, walking out of the administration office with his first paycheck.

"Did you see our paychecks?" Chung asked, holding up a slip of paper.

"Yeah, pathetic, isn't it? Only $1,900 a month. It isn't worth it."

"Are you kidding me? This is the most money I've ever made in my entire life!"

"You serious? What, have you been living in a third-world country?"

"Not anymore. Now I'm getting real money."

"Yeah, you're getting raped is more like it."

"Now this place is all about making money," he said, walking away.

Attention Staff:
Valley Fever is here. The prison has reported 3,000 cases of Valley Fever. Explanations for the spike have included residential development and changes in weather patterns causing the increases in fungus.

After a few weeks I felt like I had gotten the program down pretty well in the Ding ward. Actually, the program seemed to run itself. The officers didn't even wear their personal alarms; they felt the threat against them was so minimal. Officers thought the alarms looked stupid, too—like garage door openers from 1975.

Most officers placed their alarms in the desk or took the batteries out so they would not hit the alarm by accident if they fell off their chair while sleeping. A baton falling out of its holder and crashing to the ground would bring cheers from the inmates, as would an accidental alarm. The Ding atmosphere was so mellow that officers routinely slept in chairs on the dayroom floor with the inmates roaming around. Officers would never sleep on the floor in a mainline housing unit. The daily routine was to watch the inmate porters feed and shower those inmates who never left the building on third watch. Third watch was from 2:00 p.m. to 10:00 p.m.

After count the Yard Sergeant redirected me to Building Four to work the control booth. I was the newest officer on the yard, so when the sergeant needed a "volunteer" I was always chosen. I never complained; I truly wanted to learn the job as quickly as possible. The more I learned, the more comfortable I thought I would become.

I was always eager to please. I went up top to relieve Officer Timmons. He was the officer who had stolen the pancakes. His wife had called and said she was in the hospital. Officer Timmons always played country music in the control booth on a cassette player he'd confiscated from an inmate.

The control booth was filthy, like a forgotten bomb shelter. The windows were cracked, and covered in a thick gray mold. I was overwhelmed by the number of buttons on the control panel. I wasn't sure if I could do the job without practice. I didn't want to open the wrong door to allow the inmates to rush the officers on the floor, but Officer Timmons looked eager to leave.

"Nothing happened today," Timmons said.

"Okay. Hope your wife gets better."

"What?"

"They told me your wife was sick and you have to go home. Hope it's nothing serious."

He chuckled. "Oh, that. No, I just have my girl-friend call the watch office once a month to get me out of here early on my Fridays. I'm going to get drunk. I'm not even married, dawg."

I couldn't blame him for wanting to leave. Even though the state gave us sick time, calling in sick was still frowned upon by the prison. The officers considered it "calling in scared."

Timmons left. I checked the control panel to see if there were any cell doors that weren't supposed to be open. The board was filled with so many green, red, and yellow buttons that it looked like a nuclear missile silo.

I surveyed the dayroom floor trying to imagine how pathetic I must have looked standing over the control panel, clueless to my surroundings. The dayroom was full. The inmates were busy playing cards, writing letters, getting haircuts, doing laundry, exercising, and watching TV.

Things looked normal, but no more than thirty seconds had gone by when the building alarm went off. My heart jumped. I searched the day room for the floor officers and saw they were alive, in front of the podium. The Lopez Brothers were identical twin officers who did everything together. Their nicknames were "the Torpedo Brothers," because they liked to tackle the inmates during fights. I shifted my gaze to a group of inmates fighting next to the stairs.

The Lopez Brothers emptied their MK4 cans, which held only tiny amounts of pepper spray. Each can was the size of a cough syrup bottle.

I grabbed the Mini .14 rifle and provided gun coverage for the officers, praying that they wouldn't get stabbed in the fight. I prayed I wouldn't have to fire the rifle and kill someone by accident. I prayed that if I *did* fire the rifle I'd at least kill the right person and not the officers. I felt two miles away and fifty stories above.

A prison fight does not move in a choreographed pattern. It comes out of nowhere, a cluster of flying fists.

The officers pulled out their batons. They were screaming commands at the inmates and striking them with their batons. "Get down! Get down!"

The inmates weren't getting down. I drew the rifle sight down on them, then I racked a round into the chamber. The sound was distinct. The inmates knew immediately what it was. Those fighting dropped to the floor. Everyone looked up at me. No one said a word. Silence in a prison is agreement.

I opened the back door for responding staff. Sergeant Manny Amos strolled in last and looked up at me, my rifle hanging out the tower. Amos, in his fifties, was a veteran of several prisons and known to keep a cool head. It had earned him the respect of many officers. Amos was short and stout, with acne scars on his darkly tanned face. He liked to recruit women officers to work on his yard.

"Why did you have the rifle out?" Amos asked calmly.

I wasn't sure why I had it. I had just grabbed the rifle without thinking.

"I was maintaining gun coverage for the floor staff, sir. Making sure the officers stayed alive."

"Fucking outstanding, kid. Outstanding," Amos said.

On a Level Four yard the control officer was supposed to have the rifle slung at all times, but it was cumbersome and awkward, so few officers carried it. The inmates also looked at you like you were nuts for having the rifle locked and loaded in the control booth.

Shooting in a housing unit was dangerous, because bullets would ricochet. The old shooting policy mandated the shooting of inmates engaged in a fistfight, but the new policy was to use a less violent means to get inmates to stop fighting. It was a kinder, gentler shooting policy.

The rifle was only good for extreme emergencies; otherwise, no one wanted to use it. No officer wanted to be fired or arrested for manslaughter.

I had no idea how to even begin to describe what I had just seen. I would need a few hours to calm down first. Then another hour to convince myself it had actually happened.

I felt like I was trying to identify someone in a police lineup of 20 clones. The inmates all looked the same. There was no way of telling them apart unless I had been on the floor. The inmates in the fight were all young, tall, slender, fit men in their early twenties with shaved heads, wearing state-issued blue clothing; the prison had grooming standards to which everyone conformed.

"I'll have another officer relieve you in a couple of minutes, after we take care of this mess," said Sergeant Amos.

The officers spread out across the dayroom floor and systematically stripped out the inmates one by one. They were looking for weapons, blood, and any puncture marks to connect the inmates to the incident. Many times a weapon would be used in a fight and no one would ever know, because the puncture marks were so small. The victim was never eager to talk; getting stabbed was one thing, but snitching on the inmate who'd tried to kill you was a death sentence.

The dayroom was shut down and the inmates were locked back in their cells.

The inmates involved in the fight were escorted outside and placed against the center fence, to let the night air get rid of the chemical agents in their eyes. The Lopez Brothers were in a huddle trying to piece together the events of the fight, like a crime scene.

I was glad the brothers knew what they were doing. They had been involved in other prison fights. They at least knew the inmates' names and who was involved in the fight. I recognized one of the inmates, Forbes, who had tried to commit suicide a month earlier.

Anger swept over me when I found out that they were going right back to their cells with only a write-up. As long as the inmates signed a marriage chrono (a form stating they wouldn't fight again), they were free to return to their cellblock.

I protested to Sergeant Amos. "I don't get it. The inmates put the officers' lives in danger and nothing's going to happen to them?"

"There's not enough beds in The Hole. The only thing I can do is ship the inmates' property to R and R for a few weeks."

"So you take away their property, but they'll just get it back in a few days."

"I agree," said Sergeant Amos. "This is prison. You just gotta accept it."

The whole incident wasted more than four hours. The inmates got out of going to The Hole, but officers still had to write reports so the inmates couldn't come back later and try to sue us.

The staff gathered in one of the education classrooms to go over the incident.

A haggard-looking, old white inmate sat down next to me with tattooed knuckles that read, "H-A-T-E C-O-P-S." His name was Randy Boggs and he was the program clerk. Boggs was serving a ten-year sentence for selling drugs and guns for a motorcycle gang. He was nicknamed "Doc," because he once attended dental school. His eyes were sunken and his face sagged like a melted candle.

"Tell me what happened," Boggs asked.

I thought I was in the *Twilight Zone*. Giving information to an inmate? "I'm not telling you shit."

"But I'm the program clerk," Boggs said.

"So what?"

"It's okay," said Sergeant Amos. "He types all of our reports."

"You've got to be joking."

"Wish I was," said Amos.

Sensitive information was always a serious issue at the prison, yet here they were just handing it out to the inmates? The Academy had led cadets to believe that the inmates were clueless to the officers' activities. In reality, the inmates had access to all the officers' personal information, because the inmates were left alone with state computers. In fact, the department had already issued officers a letter stating that all of our personal information, including Social Security numbers, had been stolen.

The inmates were given a copy of every incident report, which had employees' full names and badge numbers. The officers were giving information that would get right back to the very inmates who had been involved in the fight.

The Academy had taught cadets to never talk to inmates about anything that pertained to official state business, but the inmates not only typed reports, they actually *wrote* officers' reports. Without the inmates, the officers would never get anything done because officers had to document every incident. An officer might spend all his time writing reports rather than doing his job. If the inmates didn't have jobs that helped the officers, the prison would fall apart; the prison relied on the inmates that much.

Attention Staff:
The department has received numerous complaints from inmates stating that there have been many times they did not understand their Miranda Rights read to them in standard English. We feel this may be due to a language barrier. Please speak in a slow and clear voice when speaking to the inmates.

The outside patrol sergeant caught me in the parking lot just as I was getting into my car. It was Sergeant Arnold. "I'm holding you over for first watch." Arnold was always working overtime.

I hung my head in defeat. "Where am I working?"

"Delta Yard," Arnold said.

It was not unusual for the outside patrol sergeant to cruise the parking lot looking for officers hiding in their cars while the front gate was frozen. This meant officers could not leave the prison grounds. Officer Timmons hid in the trunk of his car hoping not to get held over. He kept a blanket and a small television in there to help pass the time.

I headed back down to Delta Yard to count Buildings One and Two. When I got to Complex Control it was already forty minutes past ten and the officer be-hind the glass demanded to know why I was late. It was Officer Gibbs.

"Where the fuck have you been?" Gibbs demanded.

"I just got held at the gate."

"Just now?" Gibbs asked.

"Yeah, I worked third watch and got here as soon as I could."

"It's a real shame when people around here don't show up on time. It's bad for morale."

"Yes, it is."

Thankfully Gibbs had the alarms ready for me in a box. Alarms were checked twice a day to make sure that they would be ready in an emergency. Central Control had a giant map board that displayed where each alarm originated.

After that I hurried to the buildings to count. I had to count all five buildings.

I found it more difficult to count at night because most of the inmates were sleeping under a mountain of state linens. Officers were required to count a breathing body, but most officers just looked for flesh, an arm, or a leg. I tried never to shine my flashlight directly on the inmates—instead, next to the bunk; wake up an inmate enough times and he might throw a cup of shit at me during the next count.

It was hard to see anything at all in the cells and it always took a few seconds to register who and what was inside. I made it a point to always check the toilet, because the vent was directly above it; if an inmate hanged himself from it, I would see his body dangling. An inmate could be standing in front of the door and still not be visible. Many of the inmates liked to hide in the shadows under the bunk, or behind a hanging sheet. For a place as small as a prison cell, there were a lot of places to hide.

I was short on time and wasn't about to tap on each door to get the inmates to move or show me they were alive. The few inmates who were awake yelled through the door when I walked by.

"You like looking in windows, pervert?" an inmate screamed.

"Boo!" yelled another inmate. "I'm going to kill myself if you don't drink my piss!"

"Twenty-five, fifteen, three, sixty-two!" screamed another inmate, trying to make me mess up the count.

It was hard to concentrate on the numbers while ignoring the inmates. I counted each building twice just to make sure I got the count right.

My first count was off by one body because there was an inmate at the "boneyard," enjoying the weekend with his wife. Inmates not serving a life sentence were allowed conjugal visits in single-story apartments; they could even bring their kids for the weekend. There was an officer assigned to prepare the rooms and inventory the state-approved items. There was no list to tell the officers which inmate was out to court or on a transport or at the boneyard; officers relied on the inmates to tell them. This time the inmate's cellie had tried to make a body under the blankets in the hopes of getting an extra food tray in the morning. I had to re-count the building.

I wrote a quick memo for the bad count and walked it over to Complex Control. As I pressed the button to get back on Delta Yard, I was pushed from behind into the gate. I swung around. Officer Crocker grabbed me by the throat. He was the same officer who had yelled at me my first day. I gasped for air.

"Are you fucking my girlfriend?" Crocker demanded.

I threw off his hands and pushed him back. Crocker lunged forward. I stepped out of the way and he fell to the ground.

"I don't even know who your girlfriend is!" I said, trying to re-compose myself.

He looked at my name tag. "Wait, you're not Miller."

"No, I'm not!"

Crocker stood up. "Sorry, dawg. Look, please don't tell anyone. This bitch has got me twisted."

He turned and hurried off. I never saw him again.

The yard gate buzzed open. I stood for a moment, still shocked by the sudden attack. I collected my thoughts and walked toward Building Two. Counting the buildings at night also increased an officer's chance of finding the inmates having sex. Many inmates had their own house "wife" or "*chavalo*," which meant "kid" in Spanish. These inmates were the private property of other inmates and could be bought, sold, or rented for the night.

Almost every officer feared finding the inmates having sex, because some weren't shy about exposing themselves to officers. I knew my time would come. It happened to everyone who worked at the prison. It was common to see the inmates together on their bunks. Many inmates were homosexuals out of circumstance. They might be having sex with their cellmate but they truly believed they were still faithful to their wives; it was kept a secret because no one wanted to talk about it.

Just before I finished the last count I surprised two inmates having sex. One of them seemed more surprised than I was. He jumped off the bunk completely naked and ran to the cell door.

"It's not what it looks like!" he screamed. "I'm just gay for the stay!"

7

BUST
A GRAPE

Attention Staff:
In response to the rising concern regarding the possible use of biological weapons, specifically anthrax, against the citizens of the United States, we have prepared some information to help you better identify anthrax. If you suspect that you have come into contact with anthrax, gently set it down and walk away.

The visiting officer position sounded like an easy job; after all, who would want to visit convicted criminals? I expected one gray-haired lady, pleading with her son to tell her where he had hidden the money from the bank robbery.

I was not prepared for the thousands of visitors who showed up to see the inmates.

Each yard had its own visiting room, which looked like a high-school cafeteria. Two officers were assigned to each visiting room. They sat on a slightly elevated platform, and watched over hundreds of inmates and visitors sitting at tables.

My partner was Officer Haggerty, the former stripper. She had ten years in and owned an avocado farm. Every few minutes she would let out a horrible, hacking smoker's cough.

"I thought the inmates were shackled down behind glass."

"Non-contact visits are only for the inmates that have disciplinary problems," Haggerty replied.

"That doesn't sound so bad for the inmates."

"Nope. The inmates also get family portraits."

"Where do they take them?"

She pointed to a corner. "There's an officer over there who takes them."

"The inmates look like they're going to the high school prom."

"Yeah, they get dressed up. They call it 'getting bonarooed.'"

"Bonaroos" were, typically, a nicely pressed blue shirt with heavy starch, ironed pants, and a spit-polished shine on the tips of the inmate's brown boots. The word came from a 1970s album by New Orleans singer Dr. John. It means, "A really good time." The word *bon* is French for "good," and *rue* is "street." In other words, "the best on the streets." The inmates were getting dressed up to visit and have a good time.

"What's our job besides sitting here?"

Haggerty coughed and spat in the trashcan. "The number-one priority for visiting officers is to look for visitors trafficking drugs to the inmates."

"What's the second?"

"Look out for inmates and visitors having sex."

"In *here*?"

"It's pretty common," said Officer Haggerty. "The visit gets terminated if they can't keep their paws off one another."

"I really can't blame the inmates."

"Yeah, but it's a little embarrassing for the officers to have to pull them away from each other in front of their children. Besides, they have the boneyard."

"So, what are the inmates allowed to do?"

"They can sit next to their family, hold hands, and kiss briefly."

"Just long enough to swallow a balloon full of good dope?"

"Pretty much."

Haggerty shined her flashlight on Inmate Robles, who quickly pulled up his pants. His girlfriend jumped up from her kneeling position. They both sat back down at their table.

"Keep your pants on!"

I had always wondered how drugs got into the prison, much as I wondered how inmates got their hands on a tube of Revlon mascara or blush. The majority of contraband flowed into the prison through visitors, because they were not searched.

Visitors weren't criminals. They were citizens of the community; they had constitutional rights. They couldn't be searched without probable cause. The visitors weren't even patted down during their visits.

A cursory search was done on all visitors by an officer. They had to take off their shoes and hats, and walk through a metal detector that, most of the time, didn't work. The metal detector could only pick up contraband with metal in it; it was useless against narcotics. Women were allowed to carry clear plastic purses with a maximum of thirty dollars in small bills for the vending machines inside, but that never stopped the flow of illicit cash into the institution. Wigs and hats were prohibited, because an attorney had used them to smuggle a gun into a prison in the 1970s.

If the visitors were suspected of introducing contraband, they were asked their permission to be searched by an officer. Female visitors suspected of bringing in drugs had to be searched by female officers; male officers were prohibited from searching female visitors. Most of the contraband was smuggled in by female visitors or their children. Because it was a male prison, most visits were made by women.

"It's usually a female," said Haggerty. "Female suspects are taken into the women's restroom and politely asked to strip out."

"What if they refuse?"

"Police are contacted. Children are used as drug mules because their parents think they're less suspicious. If the visitor refuses a search and there is probable cause, then a search warrant has to be issued from a judge."

"That's time-consuming."

"Yeah, so most of the time the visitor is just escorted off the premises, to save the prison the risk of being sued. Then the officer has to file the proper paperwork in order for the inmate to lose visitation rights, and document that the visitor should be prohibited from coming onto prison grounds."

"How long are they banned for?"

"A year. Then they can petition to come back and visit the same inmate they tried to bring in drugs for. They always come back."

Working the visiting room made officers realize that the answer to the recidivism rate lies within the subculture of visiting. It was a breeding ground for criminals.

Virtually any inmate's incarceration could be tracked back to some type of abuse or neglect from a dysfunctional family. His life had little meaning. He had dropped out of school and abused drugs. He gravitated toward gangs. A street gang gave him a sense of security and made him feel important, for once. It gave him a sense of self-worth. The inmate's parents gave up on him, his teachers gave up on him, the community gave up on him, and then the state gave up on him. The gang never did.

Being a criminal filled a void and gave the inmates a sense of self-worth. In prison there were thousands of inmates who felt the same way and shared the same pain.

Once incarcerated, most inmates were simply trying to fit in and find some respect. Respect they never got. More than anything the inmates talked about getting "respect" from other inmates and from the officers. The inmates didn't have a clue as to what respect was, but they wanted it. The inmates were flattered when you called them "gangsters," because it gave them an identity. They were the last gladiators in a new Rome.

"Prison is only effective if the person being incarcerated has something to lose before getting arrested," said Haggerty. "If he was running with a gang on the streets and didn't have a job, then prison is a great place to be, because all his friends are there."

Children were allowed to visit and witness prison in a controlled environment that glorified it as a fun and safe place to be. This was how the cycle continued through generations. The children saw their family members there, and friends' family members; thus it only reinforced the idea that prison was a righteous place to become a man. The children thought prison was perfectly normal, and the families thought prison was perfectly normal too. It was no wonder that teenagers were getting locked up for life in adult prisons; they were trying to impress the very same adults they looked up to.

The children got to see their dads in prison when they were all dressed up, and take pictures with them, like they were superheroes. The kids felt like they were part of one big happy family for the day, and why shouldn't they? Mommy and Daddy weren't fighting like they used to because they didn't see each other much anymore. The kids got to play with all the toys provided by the state, and they could buy candy, cake, chips, ice cream, and sodas from the state vending machines. At the end of the day, Daddy would wave goodbye and smile as he slipped behind a door with a friendly correctional officer in tow.

What the kids never saw behind that door was that Daddy got stripped out and searched for contraband by the guards. The kids didn't see Daddy go back to his housing unit and his eight-by-ten prison cell. They didn't see Daddy have sex with his lover or get stabbed on the yard for snitching on another inmate. There's nothing that tells the children that prison is wrong, because the parents certainly aren't going to waste their time talking about it during a visit.

"Prison is just a business to the inmates, and visits are a part of the hustle because visitors are customers and distributors," said Haggerty. "I'll show you. Hey, Jenkins."

Haggerty got the attention of one of the inmate porters sweeping the floor next to the snack machines. Inmate Randy Jenkins was doing ten years for armed robbery.

"What do you need, Haggerty?" asked Jenkins.

"How do you like prison?"

"I'd rather be somewhere else," Jenkins said.

"Like where?" Haggerty asked.

"I like the prisons up north. The officers let us drink pruno. The inmates get more things from the state. Like at Christmas, we got boxes of tobacco with rolling papers. I had a lot of fun my first term, back in 1985."

"What do you mean you had fun?"

"I mean I had a great time. All my friends were there, and I didn't have to listen to my old lady bitch about me getting a job and paying child support."

"What do you do about money?"

"I ain't gonna bust a grape over it. I got ways to get my money in here and out there."

"Thanks, Jenkins," said Haggerty. "That's all I wanted to know."

"No problem," Jenkins said.

Haggerty rolled her eyes. "That's prison life."

"I can't imagine why anyone would want to be with an inmate," I said. "Can't these women do better than a man who can't provide for them?"

"They like the drama. It's all they have," said Haggerty. "They don't know any better."

"Well, I'd be pissed waiting in those long lines."

Cars loaded with visitors lined up outside the prison as early as ten o'clock the night before the doors opened. Some of these visitors travel hundreds of miles just to be turned away, because the yard was slammed, or the inmate lost his visiting privileges.

"The inmates are safe from criticism while they're here," said Haggerty. "They feel comfortable around one another and comfortable with their surroundings. No one wants to make their incarceration any worse than it is."

Haggerty suddenly stood up and jumped over the counter with the grace of a ballet dancer. She charged Inmate Robles, who was kissing his girlfriend. Haggerty grabbed Robles by the throat and choked him.

"Spit it out, Robles!" demanded Haggerty.

Haggerty applied more pressure to Robles' neck. Inmate Robles spat out a small plastic baggie of heroin. Haggerty let go of his neck and Robles sucked in a deep breath. I grabbed Robles' arm and placed him in handcuffs. Haggerty turned to Robles' girlfriend.

"Give me the rest of the dope," Haggerty demanded.

"I ain't got no dope on me, bitch."

"Don't lie to me," sneered Haggerty. "I'll drag your ass into the bathroom and search your pussy faster than you can blink."

The visitor stuck her hands down her pants and pulled out five more plastic baggies of heroin. She tossed them on the floor.

"Are you happy now, you fucking dyke?!"

"Yeah, I'm happy." Haggerty turned to the rest of the room. "Visiting hours are over!"

We shut down the visiting room and the other visitors exited grumbling. I followed Officer Bates into a back room to help him strip out ten inmates. The same Bates I had met my first day at the front gate. Bates had been put in visiting as punishment by the warden after crashing his car while drunk and then fleeing the scene of the accident. He left his badge in the car, and the police called the prison. Bates was waiting for his investigation to be completed; until then he was stuck in visiting.

"What do we do now?" I asked Bates.

"We've got to get these inmates back on the yard as soon as possible. Shit, I barely look at them."

"Aren't we supposed to search them?"

"There's no way we're going to search all of them thoroughly. It's basically a joke and the inmates know it. They just strip down and put their clothes back."

"It kind of defeats the purpose, doesn't it?"

"Hell, we're still getting paid," shrugged Bates. "What the fuck do I care?"

There wasn't much I could do. When two officers disagreed, one of them had to give in. If Officer Bates wasn't going to do his job, then neither was I. I kept my eye on the door and listened to Inmate Jenkins talk to another black inmate.

"How was your visit, fool?" Jenkins asked.

"My baby's mama done had anotha crumb snatcher."

"Now how the fuck you got anotha kid from that ho? You been down wit me two years, fool!"

The inmate stopped for just a moment, then smiled. " But hey, ain't nothin' gonna ruin my day. I'm a daddy!"

8

SERIOUS AS A HEART ATTACK

Attention Staff:
Corrections is again working to bring hundreds of children to visit their incarcerated fathers. This event will help strengthen the bond between father and child, and that's especially important when these men are released from prison.

was working a double shift in Building A4 the next morning when I was contacted by phone to report to the Security Squad room. The Security Squad was a team of officers who functioned like the Internal Affairs division inside the prison. Their main purpose was to investigate prison crime. Many officers despised the Security Squad because they kept information from the officers rather than share it. The Squad wanted to take credit for any narcotics arrest or gang information made by an officer. The call sounded urgent. I couldn't think of anything I might have done to warrant such a request.

The Squad room was next to the inmate assignments office. I looked down the hallway, hoping no one would see me go in. Any officer seen going into the Security Squad room was quickly labeled a snitch by other officers. The last thing I needed was everyone looking at me sideways, thinking I was a snitch.

I knocked on the door and Sergeant Arnold opened it. He pointed to a chair in the corner of the room.

"Sit down over there. I have some paperwork for you to sign."

"What kind of paperwork?"

"For a random drug screening," Arnold said.

It was a relief to hear I had to take a drug test; it meant I would get a few hours away from the prison.

"Where do I go for that?"

"That's not my problem. I'm just here to issue you the paperwork. Now, I have to read you a letter advising you of your legal rights. This is to inform you that all new officers must comply with the random drug policy set forth by the state. Veteran officers are exempt from testing pursuant to the union contract."

"So, you don't know where I'm supposed to go?"

"Try the yellow pages," he said curtly.

"Can I get a copy of the paperwork I just signed?"

"What for?"

"Aren't I supposed to get one? It's my legal right."

He finally looked up.

"The copier doesn't have any ink and we're out of paper. They haven't signed the budget. We've been out of supplies for the last week and I don't give a fuck about your rights."

I stood up and left the Squad room. I walked to the Administration Building to check out a state vehicle. Officers were required to take a state vehicle if they left prison grounds on duty.

I was given the keys to a white Toyota truck with 200,000 miles on it, and directions to the clinic. The truck wouldn't start. The radiator was cracked and the truck overheated. I called the prison, but was unable to reach anyone so I drove my own car. I spent the next four hours waiting around in a free clinic. The clinic was packed. A female nurse in a dirty smock came out into the waiting room and handed me a plastic bottle that looked used. She escorted me to a bathroom and closed the door.

I filled the urine bottle and went back to the prison.

Upon my return, I was redirected to the Minimum Yard.

Officer Trudy Black was chubby, with long brown hair and a Cajun accent. Black greeted me at the entrance to the Minimum Yard. Level One inmates were convicted felons deemed a low-risk of escape. It didn't mean they weren't dangerous. These inmates were kept on a separate yard outside of the main prison.

"Have you ever worked Minimum Yard before?" Black asked.

"Never. But I did respond to an alarm out here once. It took about twenty minutes because it's so far."

"Was that the food fight?"

"Yes," I said. "I thought it was a mass suicide at first, then realized the inmates had been serving spaghetti for dinner."

"That was my day off, thank God. Mostly, this is just a yard full of whiners and crybabies. It's a lot different from the Level Four Yard. The inmates here have way too many privileges."

The main entrance to the Minimum Yard was just a six-foot gate with a padlock. The officer parking lot was right next to the main entrance, giving the inmates a perfect view of our cars; every inmate knew someone on the outside who had access to the Internet or the DMV. There was no gun coverage on the Minimum Yard, and there was no way to communicate with the inmates over a loudspeaker because there was no yard gunner. If there was an alarm it took responding officers from the main prison twenty minutes to get there.

"What do the inmates do out here for jobs?" I asked Black as we walked to the program office.

"They have the outside work-crew jobs and they have a contract with the city to pick up trash around the parks. They also work in the warehouse, water treatment, the recycling plant, and with the trash truck."

"That's a lot of jobs."

"Yeah, Monday through Friday there are inmates in and out of that gate all day long."

Sergeant Cameron was sitting in his office when we arrived. I had met him my first day. His dream was to be in a rock band. He was laid-back, and friendly to the inmates. He had his boots off and was scraping dead skin off the bottom of his feet into a wastebasket. I was disgusted, but I had to give him credit for throwing his dead skin in the trash instead of on the floor for the inmates to sweep up.

"Did you hear about the inmate they rolled up today?" Sergeant Cameron asked.

"No, what about him?"

"He had five golf ball-sized balloons in his ass full of heroin."

"Five? Can't be physically possible."

Sergeant Cameron laughed. "I wouldn't know. I've never had more than two at a time."

The officers' equipment was in an unlocked closet easily accessible to inmates. I grabbed my equipment and walked outside to the yard. The inmates were playing softball. I sat down on a chair in front of the program office next to Officer Black.

"This is it," said Black. "Sit on your ass and collect your state money. That's all we do."

Officer Black was right. The Minimum Yard was slow-paced. The inmates policed themselves. Rarely was there a fight, because the inmates were "short to the house—they had release dates and were eager to get home. I walked around for a bit and then went in to see how the inmates lived. I stuck my head in the dorm for a moment and spotted some inmates playing ping-pong. There was one officer assigned to each dorm to watch 200 inmates on bunk beds. That officer was sleeping on a broken chair in the office. It was Officer Beers, the same officer who got in trouble for sleeping at the hospital. He was an overtime hog who earned at least $125,000 a year.

The dorm area was the size of a gymnasium, with low ceilings. It was packed with double bunk beds, and oversized lockers with padlocks. During prison riots the inmates were known to put their locks in their socks for weapons, known as "slocks." On the Minimum Yard inmates were allowed to have their own locks to keep their property safe. The dorm area was equipped with tables and showers for the inmates. It also had a washer and a dryer, so the inmates could do their own laundry.

I heard an inmate yell my name from across the room so I quickly walked outside and closed the door. The inmate caught up to me at the program office. It was Forbes. The inmate I had taken to the outside hospital. His case was overturned in court. His points had dropped and the prison had moved him to the Minimum Yard.

"I have a family visit tomorrow. How come my wife hasn't called or contacted me?"

"I've got no idea."

"Well, can you call R and R, and see if my package is here? I've been waiting for it for like eight months."

The inmates were allowed packages from family members, up to thirty pounds.

"I'll see what I can do."

"Yeah, because this place never helps anyone out. I should sue their ass."

"That's a great idea."

Inmates were always asking officers why family members hadn't sent packages, visited them, called, or written letters. Forbes ran back into the dorm. I walked back to the program office.

"You've got to take the inmate porters to the Administration Building," said Black, leaning back in her chair. "They forgot to clean the bathrooms yesterday."

"How do I do that?"

"Just take those five inmates over by bus."

"I drive them up there alone?"

"Yeah. Just make sure you check their IDs before they leave."

I searched for the keys to the bus until finally Inmate Ortiz told me that the bus didn't have any keys. I didn't believe Ortiz, so I had him show me where the bus was and how to start it.

"We call this bus Old Bessie," said Inmate Ortiz.

The bus was ancient and rusted, donated to the prison by an elementary school. It had been painted white, and the ignition had been ripped out and replaced with a screwdriver. I couldn't even put the bus in reverse. Instead, I had to circle the prison in order to drop off the inmates. Inmate Ortiz had been helpful, but his true character came out as I drove toward the Administration Building.

"You're really a fucking idiot, C.O. You don't even know how to drive a bus. What a dumb ass you are." The other inmates laughed.

I slammed on the brakes and walked back to Ortiz. The inmates were always testing the officers and word would spread around the prison that I was weak if I let Ortiz get away with disrespecting me.

"What's your problem?" I asked.

"You ain't nothing without that belt on!"

I took out my pepper spray and dropped my utility belt on the floor. I tossed the can of pepper spray at Ortiz and he caught it. He looked stunned.

"Let's go right now!" I yelled.

"What do you mean? I don't want to fight you."

"Then shut the fuck up!"

"I'm sorry. I was just fooling around! Please don't write me up. I'm short to the house!"

Ortiz handed me back the can of pepper spray and put his head down. The other inmates were silent. I picked up my belt and sat back down. I had changed into a prison guard. I was no longer willing to see both sides to anything. My frustration with the prison had made me a bitter person. I was always on edge, ready to snap at anyone who questioned me in any way.

When I got back, Officer Black and I watched movies in the Art in Corrections room. The inmates were allowed to paint and take art and drawing classes. The paints and blank canvases were locked in a cage so inmates and officers couldn't steal them. The art teacher had the key.

"Where did the sergeant go?" I asked Black as she changed channels.

"He's in the chapel playing guitar with the inmates."

"Are you serious?"

"Yeah, he has a band and plays with the inmates every day. They call themselves The Convicts."

Very few officers willingly hung out with the inmates. "Does anyone know about this?"

"Oh, yeah. He has a memo from the warden. They live next door to one another."

"That sounds a little strange to me."

"Yeah, it freaks me out. I just stay away from Cameron. He's weird."

An hour before my shift ended I was redirected to the Central Infirmary for a suicide watch. Each yard had a medical room, but if the injuries were serious the inmates were taken to the Central Infirmary in an ambulance. When I arrived, Officer Timmons handed me a logbook and a small metal box. Timmons had been suspended for sleeping on duty and placed on sick relief; he was only allowed to watch inmates at the infirmary. Timmons brought a blow-up mattress with him and quickly fell asleep, later failing to answer the radio when the outside patrol sergeant came to check on him. Because the sergeant couldn't contact Timmons, he got a "hot key" to open the tower. (Hot keys were keys that gained access to restricted areas that were not carried by officers.) The sergeant pushed on the hatch, but Timmons was sleeping on top of it. The movement woke Timmons, and he quickly opened the tower window and threw the air mattress outside. The mattress landed on the barbed-wire fence and burst. It took three days for the mattress to be removed. And because the tower was right next to the main prison entrance, everyone saw it.

"I've never done suicide watch," I said. "What am I supposed to do?"

"The post orders are in the box. Just sit on him and make sure he doesn't die."

Inmate Robbins was inside the cell. I knew him from the Ding ward. He was the inmate who cried when he couldn't get blankets for his birthday party. He was pacing the cell in a circle, rattling his leg and hand restraints. All he had on was a pair of white boxers wrapped around his thighs and waist with medical tape. The door of the cell was open. I felt nervous. The inmate looked agitated.

"Why is he in full restraints?"

"Oh, they think he swallowed something. He's on potty watch too."

"What did he swallow?"

"I don't know. A razor. Anyways, I'm outta here, dawg."

Officer Timmons left. I opened the metal box: empty. I looked at the suicide watch log. There was a series of entries from the last shift:

2:00 p.m. Officer on duty. Suicide/Potty watch for Inmate Robbins. Inmate Robbins stabbed his cellmate in the neck while he was sleeping. Inmate Robbins stated his cellie snored too loud and he wanted him dead. Inmate Robbins stated he swallowed a razor. Inmate is sleeping.

2:30 Inmate is sleeping.

3:00 Inmate is awake.

3:30 Inmate was served chow. Trash collected.

4:00 Inmate banging his head on the wall. Told to stop banging his head on the wall. Inmate complied with orders.

4:30 Inmate asked for medication. Nurse gave inmate meds.

5:00 Inmate is sleeping

5:30 Inmate is sleeping

6:00 Count time.

6:30 Inmate states he wants to go back to his cell.

7:00 Inmate jumping off his toilet. Inmate told to stop. Inmate complied.

7:30 Inmate urinated on the floor. Inmate given new paper pants and suicide blanket.

8:00 Inmate drinking from the toilet. Inmate was told to stop drinking from the toilet. Inmate complied.

8:30 Inmate asleep. All secure.

9:00 Shift change. Officer off duty.

Suddenly, the inmate began screaming at the top of his lungs, "Beaners!" The medical staff rushed to the cell like they were responding to an alarm.

"What did you do to him?" demanded Nurse Tripodi.

"I didn't do anything," I said. "I just got here."

"Why is he screaming?"

"I don't know. Did you give him any meds?"

"No, not yet. I'll get him a shot," said Nurse Tripodi.

"Maybe that might help."

The nurse pointed to an object next to the toilet covered in blood. "What's that?"

There was a small plastic cylinder sitting on the floor covered in blood and feces. The inmate had defecated the cylinder and had tried to hide it. The nurse bent down and put the cylinder in a plastic bag.

"You need to check this out," Tripodi said.

"No problem."

Tripodi left, and I looked at the cylinder. It was full of tobacco. I tossed the plastic bag in the trash. I had been placed on suicide watch, not potty watch, so I wasn't about to search through an inmate's shit.

Tripodi came back a few minutes later and gave the inmate several pills that knocked him out almost immediately. I sat down. Officer Black came running down the hallway toward me.

"There's been an escape from the Minimum Yard!" she said. "We gotta go to the armory, now! Two inmates cut a hole in the fence and escaped just before the last count!"

"What about this inmate I'm sitting on?"

"Fuck him," she said.

She slammed the cell door and we took off for the armory on the other side of the prison.

The armory was where the prison kept all of its tactical weapons. It was a concrete structure that sat next to the vehicle sally port. During an escape, each officer was issued a .12 gauge shotgun and a black vest containing a map of the city, a radio, extra ammunition, and a sidearm. There was a box on the armory wall containing keys for vehicles from the motor pool. Officer Black and I checked out a state truck and drove off the prison grounds in search of the two escapees.

"Have you ever done an escape detail?" asked Black.

"No," I said. "Have you?"

"A few. Whenever an inmate escapes, the prison sets up a command post in the Administration Building

"What goes on at the command center?"

"The room is filled with administrators trying to piece together information about the escapee. The inmate's central file is pulled to find out where his parents live, or his last known address. His picture is copied off and distributed to all the officers involved in the search."

I looked at our copy. It was black-and-white and barely legible. "This picture is horrible, and the map they gave us is ten years old."

"Yeah, they haven't updated it since the last escape."

We were looking for Inmates Forbes and Ortiz. The same two inmates I had spoken to only hours earlier. They both owed $500 to Inmate Jenkins, the visiting porter, for a heroin debt. Jenkins had given them a week to pay up or he was going to kill them. They escaped right after chow. Inmate Ortiz had stolen wire cutters from the electrician the week before when he was working on the outside lights. He cut a two-foot hole in the fence behind the sergeant's office next to the trash dumpsters, and off they went.

It was eleven o'clock at night. Escape detail sounded fun, but there were miles of open desert—not to mention thousands of homes, schools, parks, and buildings. The prison didn't have helicopters or planes to search from above, because the prison didn't want the community or the media to find out. Officers loved escapes because they got to go outside the prison and act like police officers. Correctional officers weren't trained for inmate escapes at the Academy because escapes didn't happen very often. Our instructions were to sit on the corner and watch for suspicious people.

The hunt for the escapees was more like the Baja 500. Officers and supervisors were checking out state vehicles, trucks, and ATVs, and driving them across the nighttime desert. These were vehicles that hadn't been driven in years. Some vehicles were brand-new and had been forgotten in the motor pool by prison staff. A group of officers was sweeping through neighborhoods and schools with loaded weapons and little training on how to catch fugitives. As employees of the state, the officers had to be careful not to disturb the community, for fear of lawsuits or bad media press. Sergeant Arnold got excited and kicked in the front door of a family residence because he thought the escapees might be inside. He was greeted inside with a taser to his head by the homeowner. Sergeant Arnold dropped his weapon and pissed his pants. He was rushed to the hospital.

Officer Timmons mistakenly arrested a man talking on a pay phone, thinking he was a fugitive. Timmons stuck a gun to his head and forced him to the ground. The man shit his pants. He hand-cuffed the man and held him in the trunk of his car for an hour until it was confirmed he had detained an innocent man.

The prison searched frantically while the city slept. They were found four hours later hiding in a public park by the playground. Officer Duncan, my academy roommate, had transferred to the prison that day. Duncan had been praying and driving past a park when he saw two men on the swing set. Duncan stopped to question them and asked for some identification. Inmate Forbes handed him his inmate ID card along with a prison medical ducat. Duncan shouted over the radio.

"The Lord has led me to the escaped convicts!"

9

DO YOUR EIGHT AND HIT THE GATE

Attention Staff:
During these troubled times, we want to remind you that while you are on duty, your allegiance is first and foremost to the state. Your primary duty is carrying out the department's business with your best foot forward. That means being considerate to those who may depend on you at the job site. It means adhering to our work schedules, using state equipment and state time for only state business, and getting permission before taking time off work.

S ergeant Arnold called me at home demanding to know why I wasn't at work. Veteran officers were smart enough not to answer their home phones.

"You're scheduled to work Bravo Yard today!" screamed Sergeant Arnold.

"No, it's my day off."

"I've got you working on the yard right now. You're late!"

"But the movement sheet didn't say anything when I left yesterday. I've already worked five days straight."

"It was posted an hour ago."

"How am I supposed to know that, when I work third watch and get off work at 10 p.m.?"

"I don't give a fuck! You need to check the board daily!"

"I live two hours away."

"That's not my problem, that's *your* problem. Are you coming to work or not? I'd be happy to mark you down AWOL. There are plenty of other officers that will take the overtime while I dock your pay."

The employees' contract clearly stated that officers received two days off after working five consecutive days. I was finding out supervisors didn't care about the contract.

"Yeah, I'll be there," I finally said.

I raced to work. My position was Bravo Yard recreational officer. The name was derived because the recreational officer had the key to the sports equipment cage that sat on the recreational yard for the inmates. It was a locked cage filled with basketballs and soccer balls.

I made my way through two doors and up onto the roof until I reached the catwalk. I passed by the yard gunner shack above the program office, and reached a small roof hatch above the chow hall. I didn't have the key, so

I banged on the hatch a few times until the officer down inside pushed open the door.

Officer Lars stuck his head out. "What's up, homie?" It was good to see a familiar face.

I descended a ladder and closed the hatch door behind me. I hadn't seen officer Lars since graduation. Lars had already tasted action, firing the 37mm block gun in the chow hall during a disturbance a few weeks earlier. I felt lucky being in the presence of a new officer who hadn't frozen when faced with a serious situation.

Lars and I stood perched above the inmates on a concrete balcony to provide gun coverage. I looked down. There were three officers on the floor. One officer stood next to a slot where the food trays came out and made sure that the inmates didn't take more than one tray. On the other side of the wall, the kitchen officer watched the steam line, making sure the inmate workers didn't steal food.

An officer watched the line of inmates being seated and directed them where to sit. Each table was made of steel, and seated four inmates. "I pity the officers on the floor," said Lars. "Locked inside. If the chow hall kicks off they'd have to kiss their asses goodbye."

The inmates knew the procedures for chow, but every day was a constant struggle to make sure they weren't stealing food. There was so much movement going on, and so little time to feed all the inmates, that some inmates simply got back in line and no one noticed them. Even if I did spot someone in the food line twice, there was no way to call down to the officers on the floor to stop them; the phone didn't work.

After chow, I got my yard equipment and met up with the yard officers. The yard gunner announced "open yard" over the loudspeaker and the inmates started to pour out of the cellblocks. Officers made their rounds on the yard; I stayed close to them.

The administration was having a meeting in the program office; they stopped to survey the yard. Captain Woodes called me over from behind the fence to talk. Captain Woodes was a six-foot-two woman with purple hair, long purple nails, and purple lipstick. Woodes had been fired for living with a parolee, but was able to get her job back when the prison lost its time constraints on the investigation. She was eating a large bag of potato chips. Woodes scratched her head for a moment and then stuck her hand in the bag of chips. "Do these inmates look grouped up to you?" Woodes asked, scanning the yard like a hunter. She had mistaken me for a veteran officer.

I certainly didn't know the answer. The inmates always looked grouped up to me. The inmates separated themselves on the yards by race and re-grouped in a constant power struggle.

In time I would learn the warning signs of a prison riot, such as the yard being too quiet, the inmates coming out "suited and booted" (wearing thick layers of clothes in the summertime for body armor); inmates refusing to leave their cells; and inmates stocking food supplies in preparation of a lockdown. The best way to answer a supervisor was always with another question.

"Do they look grouped up to you?"

"Yeah, I think they do," she said. "What do you think they're up to?"

"Being criminals?"

She wasn't paying much attention to me, otherwise she would have caught on that I didn't have a clue. She studied the yard for a few more seconds and then headed back into the program office, satisfied that I knew what I was doing.

The mornings were always freezing, but by the afternoon it was easily 110 degrees. The blistering sun rose right over Three Block and straight into the face of the observation gunner, making it difficult for him to see past the first fence ten yards in front of him. He was at an additional disadvantage because he had to lean his body halfway out of the booth just so he could get a clear view below. It was like watching a game in a crowded stadium from nosebleed seats full of inmates. If you didn't know the inmates, they just looked like blue dots. The gunner was watching everything and at the same time watching nothing, because there was too much movement for the brain to register.

Each yard was different and operated differently, depending on the supervisors. Bravo Yard was the worst yard because it had the most incidents. Officers called in sick just to get out of working on Bravo Yard. Officer Billy Gaines had a thick beard, and Officer Juan Rodriquez had his right eyebrow pierced.

"Doesn't anyone say anything about your beard?" I asked Officer Gaines.

"Shit, these guys are just happy they can find someone to work this yard. See that one by the handball courts wearing the wife-beater?"

"Yeah," I said. "What about him?"

"He's here for raping a dog. The cops had to shoot him five times just to get him off of the dog. We've got some sick fucks out here. Do your eight and hit the gate on this yard." That meant do your shift and go home as soon as you could.

We converged on a table full of inmates playing cards and asked to see their inmate IDs. It was impossible to know the status of every inmate on the yard, and many of them were let out of their housing blocks by accident.

"Fuck that shit, fool," said Inmate Barnes, wearing a torn white shirt over his head for a do-rag. "Why you pickin' on us? There's plenty of tables to shake down. Shake the spot, pigs." Inmate Barnes was twenty-one years old, serving a twenty-year term for armed robbery and kidnapping. "Shake the spot" meant "leave us alone."

As I quickly surveyed the yard it became clear that all inmate eyes were on us, waiting for our next move. We were outnumbered. There were only six officers on the yard, watching more than a thousand inmates. The inmates didn't take kindly to our interruption while they were playing dominoes.

"Just gotta do our job," said Officer Gaines, referring to Captain Woodes standing by the chapel door with a camera crew from the local news.

"Oh, I see, politics 'n' shit. I thought the po-lice be trippin'!" said Inmate Clifford Brown, wearing headphones so big he looked like an air traffic controller. Inmate Brown was ten years into his thirty-year sentence for mayhem. He had chewed the ear off of his neighbor.

The inmates at the table looked to their gang leader, known as the "shot caller," to see what to do next. Inmate Clarence Starks was forty-three and weeks away from paroling. He had done ten years for second-degree murder. Inmates rarely made a move without his consent. He nodded his head and the rest of the inmates at the table stood up like robots, putting their arms out for the officers to pat them down.

When we walked away I asked Officer Gaines why we hadn't conducted much of a search.

"Well," he said, "from the other end of the yard it looks like we're doing our jobs, and that's all that matters. The more time we take talking to the inmates, the better."

"Yeah, but we might have found some contraband if we'd stripped them out or searched under their table."

"I'm more concerned with keeping a shank out of my throat than I am with shaking down a table full of retards. The inmates might have taken it as disrespect."

Attention Staff:
A state prison inmate here is in stable condition after castrating himself with a can opener. Effective immediately inmates will no longer be allowed to possess can openers, which are now considered contraband.

I partnered up with Officer Gaines later on and patrolled the south end of the yard next to the basketball courts. He had been working on Bravo Yard for three years and was eager to train me. Most veterans didn't want to take the time to train new officers but Gaines seemed to always be positive. Gaines pointed to two inmates shaking hands.

"Each time the inmates come in contact with each other they're passing something along, either information or contraband. I really don't care if these fuckers stab one another, but God forbid they stab one of us. Just be aware that they have weapons on them right now."

More than half the inmates had weapons in their rectum or on them at all times when they were on the yard. Usually they held on to them for two weeks and then passed them to one of their homeboys. On the yard, officers were outnumbered both by inmates and by weapons. Gaines stopped walking and scanned the yard.

"It's going to go off any second now," whispered Gaines.

"What's going to go off?"

"The yard. I can feel it coming," he said.

"Feel what?"

A panic set over me. The fear of dying was so overwhelming that I wanted to dig a hole and hurl myself into it. There was no place to go. Everywhere I looked there were convicted criminals. It was the first time I felt like it was a real war, and it was either me or the inmates.

"There it goes!" Gaines yelled.

Gaines banked to my right. I tried to follow, but I fell the second I pivoted my foot. The alarm sounded. The yard gunner ordered the yard down. Inmates rushed past me like stampeding buffalo. One of the inmates punched me in the back of my head and I went down, without seeing who had done it. I landed in a patch of fresh mud and slipped trying to get back up. The grass on the yard was sparse and the nighttime sprinklers turned the yard into a mud pit every morning. The sprinklers were usually broken from the inmates pulling them apart to make weapons. That day parts of the yard were flooded.

I blacked out for a moment and then jumped to my feet and ran toward the basketball courts. I could hear nothing. I was stunned. The blood in my body dropped to my feet, turning them into dead weight. My vision seemed like the shutter of a camera, clicking frame by frame.

There had been a cluster of inmates fighting, but when the yard was ordered down only four inmates remained standing. There were three inmates beating another inmate with their fists. The rest of the inmates were down on the ground, watching the fight. Officer Gaines was pepper-spraying the aggressors while the victim struggled back to his feet, blindly swinging his arms like he was being attacked by angry birds. The gunner shot off smoke grenade rounds that whizzed by my head. He continued to scream over the loudspeaker for the noncombatant inmates to get down, and directed the other yard staff to the fight. I choked on the smoke.

The yard was deathly quiet. My heart rate tripled in a matter of seconds; I was surprised it didn't explode.

Officer Gaines pepper-sprayed the three inmates again. They fell to the ground. Gaines dropped his spray and pulled out his baton. The inmate victim stumbled around the yard like a wounded animal. I ran over to him and aimed my pepper spray can at him. I recognized Calvin Bowers, known as "Big Boy," from Building One.

Big Boy was the biggest inmate on the yard. He weighed 500 pounds, and had one eye that looked east, so you never knew when he was looking at you. He was clumsy and slow, and the other inmates often took advantage of him.

"Get down!" I ordered.

I pushed the yellow button on the top of the can but nothing happened. I pushed down again, harder this time, and a thin stream of liquid sputtered out a few inches, like a defective squirt gun. Big Boy was already blinded and couldn't see that my pepper spray didn't work, but all the other inmates on the yard could. I felt naked knowing that my only weapon left was a baton.

"Get on the ground!" I yelled.

"Please don't spray me, please!" Big Boy pleaded.

"I said, get down!"

The prison code of inmates made it so he couldn't get down. To save his honor, even after getting jumped by three inmates, I was going to have to take him down so that he could keep his "rep" on the yard.

I could hear the jingle of keys and the pounding footsteps of responding staff. It was the best sound I had ever heard in my life. The cavalry was finally on its way.

Fellow officers laid into Big Boy and hosed him down from all sides with pepper spray like they were washing a car. Big Boy fell to the ground screaming in agony.

Officer Lars quickly cuffed Big Boy and rolled him over on his side so he wasn't suffocated by his own body weight. I turned around to check if any other inmates had advanced in my direction, but they were still down on the ground.

Officer Gaines walked over, slipped off a black leather glove and pulled a pack of cigarettes out of his pocket. He lit a cigarette and sucked in a breath of smoke in a strangely relaxed way. I bent down to search Big Boy.

"Don't touch him, he's got blood on his jacket," Gaines said, in a swirl of smoke.

I took a closer look. The inmates' jackets were dark blue, almost black. It was hard to see that Big Boy's jacket had fresh splatters of blood on it.

"I've been stabbed," cried Big Boy.

Gaines handed me some latex gloves. "Put these on and search him."

I searched Big Boy and pulled up his shirt. He had three puncture holes in his abdomen.

Big Boy was taken to the hospital. The yard was slammed and the inmates locked in their cells. The aggressors' property was rolled up, and they were placed in The Hole. I spent the rest of the shift writing my report.

"What were they fighting about?" I asked.

"Big Boy didn't pay his debts," said Gaines. "They found a shank over by the tables. He was supposed to die today."

"Good thing it wasn't us."

"You said it, brother."

My shift ended and I turned in my equipment. When I tried to go home, Sergeant Arnold wouldn't let anyone off the yard because there was a sit-down on Alpha Yard. Inmates often held sit-downs to protest the conditions of the prison. The inmates knew if they had a sit-down instead of a riot, it was a lesser charge, and they wouldn't lose their privileges.

Equipment had been checked out of Central Control and the only items left were a few chemical-agent hand grenades. I attached two of them to my belt and went to Alpha Yard. When I got there the inmates were standing around the center of the yard like they were at a concert in the park. Captain Woodes and a few sergeants were standing off to the right side, negotiating with two inmates. Each yard had inmates who were elected by other inmates to be the spokesperson for the inmates on the yard. They were known as the Men's Advisory Council, or M.A.C. Each race had a cabinet of members for the M.A.C. reps. There was a president all the way down to a secretary, and they were voted in by other inmates.

There were a dozen officers leaning against the program office wall on the other side of the yard fence. Half of the officers looked bored, the other half looked like they were ready for a war. I spotted Officer Gaines and went over to talk to him.

"What's going on?"

"The captain wants to wait things out so that no one gets hurt. They don't want us to waste any of our equipment. The budget hasn't been passed yet. The good news is the union president got us some food while we wait."

"What do the inmates want?"

"They want the two officers in Three Block removed because they constantly argue with each other. They're also demanding better food, better clothing, better medical, better programs, and ice cream at every meal."

When darkness fell, giant floodlights were brought onto the yard by truck, so officers could see the inmates. The colder it got, the fewer demands the inmates made; they wanted to go inside, where it was warm. After four hours Captain Woodes and the inmates came to an agreement. She was considered weak, always catering to the inmates' demands. Captain Woodes had thirty-five years with the state and was trying to promote to associate warden. She promised to remove the officers from the cellblock if the inmates went back to their cells; she further promised that no inmate would be written up for the sit-down. The inmates agreed.

The officers were instructed to sweep the inmates into the housing units. There were a dozen officers in each housing unit, but even with all that staff present, it still took the same amount of time to lock up the unit. I was the only officer chasing the inmates into their cells in Three Block. The other officers watched from down in the office or at the podium.

When the yard was locked down Captain Woodes had all the officers hold hands and pray on the basket-ball court. Then she made a speech.

"Praise Jesus! I want to thank everyone," said Captain Woodes. "The important thing is that no one got hurt. I know you thought I was soft, but I've been in this business for thirty-five years and things have changed. It's about safety now. It's about going home to our families. Now, I'm going to need everyone to write a report. No one leaves the yard until I get those reports."

A few officers groaned and we all marched back to the Program Office. Even though I had just written a report on Bravo Yard, I had to write another report because it was a separate incident. I was exhausted and just wanted to go home. I quickly scribbled down a few lines to give to Sergeant Arnold to sign off.

Sergeant Arnold was in his office surrounded by officers scrambling to get hold of the boxes of food that had just arrived. He was shoving a ham sandwich into his mouth and wiping his hands on his uniform when I gave him my report.

"I'll look at this later. Get something to eat first," insisted Sergeant Arnold.

"I'd really just like to get that report signed off so I can go home. I've been here for twenty hours."

"Just take a sandwich before they're all gone," Arnold insisted.

"I'm not hungry,"

Sergeant Arnold was stunned. "But it's free."

10

602 DEEZ NUTZ

Attention Staff:
As a result of numerous incidents regarding inmate complaints based on violation of the confidential legal mail process, it is necessary to reiterate department policy regarding the handling of inmate mail. Staff is reminded that failure to follow departmental policy is a violation of case law as well as our own regulations. Searches of legal mail must be conducted in the presence of the inmate to whom it is addressed and may not be read by prison staff.

Most officers didn't want to work in Administrative Segregation, or Adseg, because they thought it was too hard. They didn't want to have to serve the inmates chow; they just wanted to watch them walk to chow. I liked The Hole immediately because all the inmates were in their cells and weren't allowed to roam the tiers and dayroom. The Adseg officers wore green protective stab-proof vests with Velcro across the middle. Most of the vests were old and held together with duct tape, but it gave me a safe feeling when I walked around the prison in mine. The Adseg officers bloused their jumpsuit pants, wore combat boots, and carried two sets of handcuffs and a Leatherman utility tool on their belts. The officers always greeted the incoming inmates in the rotunda with a speech. On the mainline it was impossible to talk to the inmates in the rotunda because other inmates were always going in and out of the housing unit. Inside Adseg there was no inmate movement, so officers had time to assess the inmates' personalities. The Adseg officers' speech was always the same.

"Leave us alone and we'll leave you alone. Don't ask for bed moves, mail, yard, showers, or canteen. If you need something, write it down. Don't yell out for officers to come to your door."

Adseg ran smoothly on third watch. The rest of the prison was micromanaged by poor, inexperienced supervisors who were scared of the inmates. They showed favoritism to a few select officers. The biggest complaint that officers had was being led by a poor supervisor. Good officers waited to be transferred or promoted, or simply quit.

There was nothing that I wanted more than partners I could rely on and put my trust in. The officers in The Hole had a good work ethic and were loyal to each other.

They were the only officers who waited for each other before work and after shift change. I entered Adseg and signed into an isolation log. Anyone entering or leaving Adseg had to sign in and out so that a record could be kept.

I noticed immediately that there were no clocks in Adseg, because the inmates did not have dayroom privileges. Since Adseg was a housing block for inmate punishment, clocks were seen as a luxury, and forbidden. Inmates were prohibited from wearing watches because all property was taken away upon entering. The inmates were constantly asking the officers what time it was.

I was greeted by Officer Felix. He was thirty-five, tan, had slicked-back hair, and an easy grin. Felix had worked for a collections agency before joining the department. He had five years in the Department of Corrections. Felix loved to joke around. He was always positive and willing to take on any challenge. I liked Officer Felix because I rarely saw him get mad. He seemed the epitome of calm, cool, and collected. I felt safe working next to him. He was a born leader, but had no interest in promoting up the ranks.

Felix was clearly in charge of the officers in The Hole.

"How long have you been at the institution?" Felix asked.

"Five months."

"We got another fish," Felix announced to the other officers. "Usually they put veterans in here. I wonder why they chose you."

"I don't know. I've never worked in The Hole."

"Are you looking at my dick?" asked Felix.

"No. Why would you ask me that?"

Felix slapped my shoulder. "I'm just fucking with you. It's a joke."

"Okay. Thanks for telling me, I guess."

"And don't drink the state milk. The inmates beat off in it."

"Anything else?"

"If an inmate turns on you, take him down. If he spits on you, take him down. Don't take any shit from these inmates because they know you're new. They're preying on you right now. So flip the script on them before they get you."

"I'm getting eye raped?" "Eye rape" was a term used to describe inmates looking at officers for long periods of time.

"You bet your ass you are, so put on your eye condoms. Have you seen anyone you know here?"

"Officers or inmates?" I asked. It was a legitimate question, but I took the question personally, as if he had linked me to criminals.

"Inmates. There's a lot of staff with relatives serving time. They just don't talk about it."

I would find out through the years that many employees at the prison had relatives serving time. It was another reason to think twice before getting in an argument with an inmate. His relative might come and bitch to you later in the parking lot.

"No, I haven't seen anyone I know here. Have you?"

"I saw a guy I went to high school with. He acted like we were best buddies, so I searched his cell and found some dope and a tattoo gun."

"I thought you were friends with him."

"Not in here. I wanted him to know where he stood in this joint, and it wasn't over me."

What Felix meant was that the inmate had personal information against him, information that the gangs could use to blackmail him if he fell prey to an inmate's intimidation. An officer needed to set standards with an inmate, that he had a job to do even if he knew him. There was no such thing as friends in prison.

I made the mistake once of telling an inmate where I'd gone to high school. I told him I went to Pasadena High. The prison is so slow at times that you forget you're talking to inmates. After I told him that I went to Pasadena, every inmate called me "Pasadena," just to fuck with me.

Felix continued with his questions. "Are you married? Got a girlfriend? Is she hot?"

"What does that have to do with work?"

"Bring in a picture so I can spend some quality time with her in the bathroom."

Felix was trying to feel me out and see how I'd react. He wanted to see if he could push my buttons and get me angry. He was good at it. I didn't like talking to other officers about my personal life.

"Nothing is sacred in here," said the tower cop, listening in and leaning against the bars from above. He was a forty-five-year-old Greek with a shaved head, Tommy Pappas. He was single and had been a sergeant in the Army for twenty years. Pappas lived in Barstow, a two-hour commute each way. He loved being a corrections officer. It afforded him a lifestyle he'd never thought he'd have. He loved to sit at home and watch old war movies while drinking malt liquor. He also collected guns.

Officer Papas was a kid trapped in a middle-aged body. He loved to mess with the inmates, calling them names over the loudspeaker as they walked to the shower or the yard. If the inmates shouted back he would respond with, "You can 602 deez nutz!"

A "602" was a green form used by inmates to lodge complaints against officers.

Sergeant Pollard, on the other hand, was a high-school dropout who had labored sporadically as a steel worker to support a speed habit before coming to the prison five years earlier. Pollard felt the rules didn't apply to him. He was nicknamed "Sergeant Bi-Pollard" by the inmates and staff because he was so unpredictable. Pollard liked to do push-ups on the day room floor in front of the inmates. His cheeks were covered with pimples and his nose was crooked and beet red. He had abused steroids, had a terrible temper, and a serious case of OCD. Pollard loved to clean. While the other officers ate lunch, he mopped the floors. Pollard measured everyone by prison time, how many years an officer had on the job.

"I got a spider bite today," Pollard said, scratching his arm the first day we met. "Want to see it?"

"Sure?"

He flexed his right bicep, kissed it, and smiled. "These are my guns."

"Congratulations."

Pollard snapped and pushed me into the wall. I fell to the ground.

"Fucking fish!" Pollard screamed. He stormed off.

Felix helped me up.

"What's wrong with him?" I asked.

"He was touched in the butt hole."

Pollard bragged that he had eight years in the department when he really had five. He spent most of his time criticizing other officers he felt couldn't hack it in The Hole. He would pick fights with other officers and didn't care whether it was in front of inmates or supervisors.

Pollard had a hard time letting go of work on his days off and found it strange that people like me didn't want to talk about inmates and the prison when we were off duty. New officers were told not to take the prison home with us, but most were consumed by it. It was all they could talk about off duty.

"Pollard is a good guy," said Felix. "You gotta understand that for some guys, this job is all they got. Pollard never finished high school, and you graduated from college."

"He hates me because I went to college?"

"His old lady left him and he's broke."

"But he doesn't even know me."

"It doesn't matter. He doesn't *want* to know you."

"Why do you put up with him?"

"'Cause nobody else wants to work in here with us."

"Why not?"

"They think it's too much work."

"Imagine that."

"It's like working with Bobby Knight," said Felix. "You never know when he might snap and choke you out."

Officer Gump worked B-section, the middle row of cells, and had Tuesdays and Wednesdays off. Gump was thirty-two, with a crew cut and a thick mustache. He always had a cheesy-looking grin on his face and chewed tobacco. Gump was a lifer who loved to brag about beating inmates. His father and grandfather had both worked for the Department of Corrections. Gump had been transferred from up north after he found his ex-wife in bed with another officer. His ex-wife shot his dog and his motorcycle in a rage when he moved out of their house. He met Pollard the first day of work and the two were inseparable. Gump did anything that Pollard told him do. Gump had just returned from the program office with a puzzled look on his face. He was holding his pocket calendar.

"I don't get why they give us a holiday for Cesar Chavez. He's just a boxer, for Christ's sake."

Attention Staff:
Effective immediately all inmates housed in Administra-
tive Segregation will not exercise to organized cadence.
This type of behavior contributes to gang organizing. The
cooperation of all inmates is expected and appreciated.

The control officer checked everyone coming and going, making sure there was no unwelcome staff. Appearance was everything in prison. Officers didn't want to be caught off guard when an administrator came into the building. If the warden decided to make a surprise visit, the officers wanted to look busy. There was one officer for each tier in The Hole and two escort officers; a total of five officers and one sergeant for the entire building. The Hole was loud compared to the mainline housing units. The cellblock sounded like a row of slot machines on a casino floor; it did not absorb sound. There were no TVs or radios allowed in the cells or dayroom, so inmates had little entertainment except for constant chatter. Inmates were not allowed to receive phone calls unless it was an emergency. Usually a phone call was made from an attorney, notifying the inmate of a family member's death. Each inmate talked over the next inmate; a hundred different conversations could be heard all at once. This was known as "carnival talk." The inmates also "fished" the tiers. They attached a line made out of string to a weight—the "car," usually a shoe sole—and threw it under the door to another cell. Then the other inmate would attach whatever needed to be passed along to the car.

There was a tremendous amount of movement in The Hole without any movement at all. The inmates were confined to their cells for most of the day, but still there were wars being fought and relationships being made. The cells were almost the same as the mainline cells, except that the back windows had been blacked out with paint. All but three cells had double bunks to accommodate the already overcrowded prison lock-up unit. Cells 118, 119, and 120 were called "management" cells, because they did not have desks in them. Cell 119 had only a toilet and a sink. The inmate inside slept on the floor. Inmate Rufus Jones had been confined to cell 119 for the past two years because he received write-ups for gassing officers. A special metal box had to be placed on the food port in order to serve him meals while keeping the officers safe from assault.

The inmates relied heavily on the mail to communicate. One of my main jobs was picking up the mail bag daily and dispersing it to the inmates, but first each piece of mail had to be searched for contraband.

The mail was divided into bags that the officers carried in daily. The mail bags were left for the officers to pick up on third watch. The mail bags were always heavy. The inmates screamed for their mail the second they saw the yellow bags.

"Why do the inmates keep screaming for their mail? It comes at the same time everyday: two o'clock."

"They feel it's an invasion of their privacy," laughed Gump. "They don't want their mail searched."

The inmates would watch from their cells and see an officer with a magazine and protest that I had just dropped it off at the wrong cell. They never stopped to think that maybe another inmate had ordered the same magazine. Their thought process was childlike. If a letter didn't arrive on time from a girlfriend, I was to blame. In their minds, I was stealing their mail. The idea that someone had stopped writing them was out of the question.

"Legal mail" had to be opened by an officer in front of the inmate, and signed off with the time and date. Legal mail was mail sent to or received from the inmate's lawyer or any other government official, and stamped "legal mail" on the front. The inmates would either write "legal mail" in pen or an officer would use a stamp. Some inmates wrote "legal mail" on every envelope in the hope that they could pass on some information to their homies on the streets.

"Have you ever found contraband in the mail?" I asked.

"Yeah, someone sent in a box stamped 'legal mail,' with a false bottom," said Gump. "Inside were wire cutters, dope, and money."

Inmate Davis had his wife send the box with wire cutters. His plan was to sneak into the back of the prison, where he had made a ladder out of wooden pallets. He would cut through the first fence with the wire cutters and then climb up a light pole. From the light pole he would be able to jump over the electric wires of the fence onto the next section of the fence. He would climb down and cut through the fence to freedom. The box also had a $1,000 in it so that Inmate Davis could take a limo to the airport and fly to Mexico. He would have succeeded—if his cellie hadn't snitched him out for a shorter sentence the day before he planned to escape.

Due to the large volume, the mailroom was six weeks behind; and the inmates waited six weeks for their mail.

"What about drugs? What should I do if I find any?"

"Just let me know," said Gump. "I'll handle it."

"Have you ever found any drugs?"

He nodded. "I found a few grams of heroin mailed to an inmate member last week. They put a hit out on me."

"You're damned if you do and damned if you don't."

"Pretty much. I had to write a report and submit the dope as evidence, but the inmate still felt that I had disrespected him. He hired a lawyer to get it back."

We sorted the mail by tiers and then in numerical order starting at cell 101. Each letter was opened and searched. I opened a pink birthday card that had been soaked in perfume. Inside was a check for $500.

"That's a lot of money."

Gump looked at the check and then grabbed the card out of my hand.

"Holy shit. This is from Captain Woodes."

Captain Woodes had been fired for having sex in the chow hall with Inmate Douglas, who was serving a life sentence for rape and murder. Afterwards, Captain Woodes left her husband and two teenage sons to marry the inmate.

The biggest problem in The Hole was finding enough room to house the inmates. Bed moves were the number one problem because the inmates had to be segregated from the rest of the mainline inmates by certain criteria. The administration didn't care how it was done. Each inmate's personal file had to be checked before placing him in a cell with another inmate, because the inmates could have been in a fight ten years ago and still be enemies.

In The Hole, the inmates were issued the basics in bedding and clothing: two sheets, two blankets, two shirts, two pairs of boxers, and two pairs of socks. The inmates always wanted boxers that were size 50 or bigger, to wear as shorts. The inmates would slit open the front and sew in drawstrings to hold them up. A state-issued pen was re-purposed into a needle by pressing the tip and stretching the metal into a hook; the thread was taken from any state clothing, such as a pair of socks.

The smart inmates washed their own clothes in the shower and never turned in their laundry on Sundays, knowing that getting something worse in return was inevitable. Sometimes the building would go a month without any clean laundry, because the prison clothing workers didn't bring them over, or the prison was on lockdown. The prison was always short on laundry because the inmates tore up their clothing and sheets to make fish lines, window coverings, hammocks, room dividers, and other items. This was a direct prison violation, "destruction of state property," but inmates were rarely written up for this offense.

When the unit had them, the inmates were issued soft-soled shoes and white jumpsuits. The inmates showered three times a week and had ten hours of yard time.

There were inmates serving time in The Hole for a variety of crimes: assault, extortion, possession of drugs, theft, rape, and murder. The inmates didn't want to be in The Hole, but at the same time it was a badge of honor and gave them bragging rights over other inmates. Surviving the mainline was like getting a bachelor's degree; The Hole was like getting your master's. A weekly cell inspection was conducted to see if the inmates were maintaining a clean environment. Sergeant Pollard would fly into a rage if an inmate didn't have a clean cell, because he deemed it a direct assault against himself. He was especially concerned with the floors, although he refused to give the inmates cleaning supplies.

"I want this cell floor spotless!" Pollard demanded, walking the tiers. Officers didn't even keep their homes as clean as Pollard wanted the inmates to keep their cells.

Officers had to log the inmates' meals, trash pick-up, and time on the exercise yard. It was also noted if the inmates refused the yard privilege or meals. Officers also had to document inmate showers, which were done every other day, starting on Mondays. There were clip-boards at each end of the tier that had to be filled out every fifteen minutes to ensure that the inmates didn't commit suicide—and to show that the officers walked the tiers.

I checked off the logs daily because I was new, but the backlog date on them was more than a year old. Very few officers filled them out. With all the inmates vying for your attention it was better just to stay off the tiers.

Supplies were issued on Tuesdays. They consisted of paper, pens, pencils, tooth powder, legal documents, toilet paper, and soap. A roll of toilet paper was supposed to last the inmates one week, but they always asked for more because the tissue was used for other things, like rolling cigarettes. Tobacco was forbidden in The Hole, but somehow it found its way into the inmates' hands.

Soap bars were split in half so that no contraband could be hidden inside them. Inmates usually purchased their own soap from the canteen because the prison soap was dry and tended to cause rashes. Five sheets of plain white paper for letter writing were issued, and a pen with no casing. Any type of plastic, like a pen casing, could be melted down and made into a weapon. The inmates would roll pieces of paper over the pen filler, to give it some stability.

The pens were cheap and ran out of ink quickly, or else just didn't work at all. At one point we were out of pens for so long that I finally bought some and passed them out to those inmates who needed them most. Pencils were given out sporadically, but were about the length of one's thumb and hard to sharpen.

Visiting forms, trust-account withdrawal slips, and medical slips were in high demand. The inmates always wanted "602" grievance forms to file complaints against the prison conditions.

Some inmates became an authority on the law after they made it to The Hole, because there wasn't much else to do besides study, and a little case-law knowledge might get them off on a technicality next time they were in court. On the streets, criminals did whatever they could to victimize others. In prison, they used the system to their advantage, because they felt that they were now the victims.

Attention Staff:
This memo is being distributed to you to ensure that you are aware of your right to appeal any departmental decision, action, or policy that you can demonstrate as having adverse effect upon your welfare.

Officers made sure to wear gloves and hairnets while serving chow. Meals were served three times a day in The Hole: two hot meals and a sack lunch. The sack lunch was handed out with breakfast at 6:30 a.m. Second watch started at 6:00 a.m. and ended at 2:00 p.m., when third watch began. Because I worked third watch, I served dinner with the other officers. A steel hot cart on wheels was delivered to the back of the building by inmate kitchen workers. Officers would bring the food carts inside Adseg and place them near the wall next to cell 101. There were four pans inside the hot cart, each containing one course. The pans would be set into the serving cart. One officer would start a tray and pass it to the next officer on the chow line, each doling out portions until the tray was full. A tray was supposed to contain 2,500 calories. The calorie count was required by law. A normal-sized man would have needed two trays. Then the trays were loaded onto another cart and wheeled to the inmates' cells. Each cart could hold twenty-seven trays, but officers liked to stack the trays to see how many they could fit at once. The record was fifty-six trays on one cart without the trays falling off. All meals were eaten in the inmates' cells, served by the officers on paper trays that couldn't be melted down for weapons. Fried fish was served on Fridays, and the inmates always got ice cream on Sundays. A typical meal:

GREEN SALAD	TORTILLAS
SALAD DRESSING	VEGETABLES
MEXICAN BEANS	CHICKEN FAJITA MIX
FRESH FRUIT	SALSA
FRUIT TURNOVER	BEVERAGE
SALT & PEPPER	

My first few times feeding, several inmates dropped their trays on the floor. When I went back to the serving line to get them another tray, the other officers "clowned" me, or made fun of me for being so naïve.

"They did it on purpose because you're a fish," said Felix. "It's a game to them, to see how many times they can get an extra tray out of you. Ask for the food back before you give the inmate another tray, and see what they do."

The inmates didn't want to give back the food; even though it had been on the floor, they just wanted extra food.

Inmates would also take a food tray, throw bread or cake over their shoulder, and then act like they'd never got any.

"Officer, there's no bread on my tray!"

I would then go get the inmate another piece of bread because I assumed he was telling me the truth. Sometimes inmates threatened to kill me if I didn't give them more food.

After chow, trash was picked up, food ports were shut with padlocks, and inmates' consumption was recorded to make sure that each inmate was still alive after eating. At most meals I passed out the juice while the other officers served the trays of food. Sergeant Pollard thought he was punishing me by giving me the job, yelling each day, "You're the juice, bitch!"

A fifty-pound juice cart was wheeled around the tiers and inmates were issued one eight-ounce paper cup of juice at each meal. Most of the inmates saved their empty milk cartons from breakfast for a cup rather than use the state-issued paper cups, because they lasted twice as long. They were also bigger. The kitchen never had enough juice for all of the inmates, no matter how many times I complained. The inmates complained too, but nothing was ever done about it because the cook didn't care.

The cook wasn't a peace officer; he was free staff. He never cared about the juice, but he went ballistic if the temperature of the food was off by even one degree. The food temperature had to be above 170 degrees, otherwise, the cook was held responsible if the inmates got sick.

Each day I had to refill the juice cart with tap water from the kitchen sink, because I would run out of Kool-Aid by the time I had served the hundred inmates

on the bottom tier. They got Kool-Aid instead of juice because it was cheaper.

I had to buy instant Kool-Aid to put in the juice
cart; but there was only so much I could bring in at
once, and it was never enough to make a difference.
Over time, most inmates just gave up asking for juice,
because they knew they would never get it. I feared the
day when I would get a cup of shit in my face for short-
changing an inmate, or get gunned down on the street
twenty years later by a parolee who hadn't gotten his
juice in The Hole.

Thursday was committee day, which meant the inmates
with criminal charges had to go in front of the warden.
Sergeant Arnold usually took charge of these hearings,
providing the warden with fresh coffee and doughnuts.
Inmates were taken from their cells and put in small cages lined against the wall next to the committee room so
that they could be seen quicker. All inmates had to be escorted by officers in Adseg when they left their cells.

I was escorting an inmate into the committee
room for classification when Arnold pulled me aside to
lecture me. "You need to have your baton out at all times
when you escort these inmates."

"We don't do that on third watch."

"Well, I was in Vietnam," Arnold said.

"So? This isn't the Army. What does that have to do
with anything here?"

"If these inmates attack you, then you can defend
yourself with the baton."

"I can defend myself with my hands better than a
baton."

Officers rarely used their batons in The Hole because assaults were close-up and quick. Ground fighting

was the only useful technique. Officers had little time to respond with a baton, and at times it caused more harm than good.

"I'm a black belt in karate," Sergeant Arnold added.

"So am I," I lied.

"Have your baton out when you're in the committee room or I'll write you up. I'm in charge here."

The classification committee room was so small that the first person you'd smack in the head with your baton would be the counselor sitting next to the inmate.

Sergeant Arnold just wanted to look good. I escorted Inmate Forbes into the committee room. Inmate Forbes was the same inmate that I took to the hospital for an attempted suicide. The same inmate who had escaped from the minimum yard. He was going in front of the committee to hear what sentence he was going to get from the prison escape. Forbes hated Arnold because he wouldn't give him any pudding with his dinner. I motioned for Inmate Forbes to sit down, but he turned and kicked Sergeant Arnold in the groin. Arnold grabbed my baton and swung it back, striking the warden in the shoulder. Arnold leaped over the table in an attempt to shield the warden who had ducked under the table. I pushed Inmate Forbes down into a chair. He laughed.

"Don't worry, buddy. I like you. It's that trick-ass Arnold I hate."

Arnold especially hated when the inmates had anything covering their cell doors. The inmates had limited space in their cells, so they hung their towels on the doors and light fixtures. Arnold complained that this was a violation of the Title 15 and a safety concern, and demanded that officers enforce these regulations. The inmates left them up because they weren't going to obey any rule that petty. Arnold just wanted someone to yell at so it looked like he was being productive. Any time a new supervisor came into The Hole it was the same complaint about door coverings. It was typical prison politics, so that supervisors never had to face the real issues, like drugs, overcrowding, gangs, suicides, stabbings, AIDS, or repeated staff assaults.

After a while I learned the core of the inmate philosophy. The way the inmates looked at it was that they were criminals, and it was the job of the officers to stop them from committing crimes. The inmates were criminals, doing what they were born to do, and they were going to keep committing crimes.

I couldn't believe someone would live his life without taking responsibility for what he had done. I wasn't going to change their minds, and that was just the point. It was up to the inmates to change, because they were the ones who'd put themselves in prison. The only remorse the inmates ever showed was for getting caught.

Attention Staff:
A federal judge has overturned the policy barring inmates from receiving mail containing printed material from the Internet. Although Internet-generated mail may contain coded messages, it is now legal for inmates to possess such material.

Lawyers for the inmates had filed a lawsuit being heard before the State Supreme Court regarding the policy of separating the inmates by race. The inmates were the ones who separated themselves by race and made it difficult for the officers to house them. Inmates from different backgrounds were natural enemies and could not be forced to live together. The inmates were segregated to curb violence, but the advocacy groups were convinced that the prison system was racist. The officers were in favor of the lawsuit because it would make housing inmates easier. Inmates would not be separated by race, gangs, or medical conditions. Northern Hispanics could live with Southern Hispanics and the prisons could not be held accountable when they fought each other. Northern gangs in California fought with Southern gangs and could not be housed together in prison.

Few inmates had ever had discipline or structure in their lives, but in prison, discipline was the glue that bound them. The gangs were disciplined.

The inmates separated themselves by race on their own terms, but the media accused the prison administration of forcing the inmates to segregate. Within each of these groups were subsets from different factions off the streets—small gangs made up of groups of boys and men who had resided in the same neighborhood back home. There were more than 250 active gangs in the city of Los Angeles alone.

The gangs had a long list of rules, which some inmates posted on their cell walls and I copied down. "Always be ready for battle no matter what." "Have your property ready at all times in case you are rolled up or taken to (The Hole)." "Don't fuck your cellie." "Always answer roll call." Inmates even had roll call daily for themselves, as a morale booster. "Don't fall asleep during the day or on your watch." Inmates were always looking out for one another, in case an officer walked down the tier. "Don't get drunk and be disrespectful to others on the tier." It was common for inmates to drink pruno and cause problems for other inmates. "Don't be a snitch."

Some gang inmates were very polite and respectful, saying "thank you" and "please" in every interaction with me. Others were not as polite.

When two inmates lived together in a cell, only one left at a time; that way an officer would be dissuaded from doing a cell search because the cell wasn't empty. Officers didn't want to listen to an inmate argue with them over cell searches. It was easier to search a cell when both inmates were on the yard.

Every time a new inmate came through The Hole, the gangs demanded paperwork to prove that he wasn't a snitch or a child molester. The worst thing an inmate could be in prison was a child molester. Most of the inmates felt that they had been robbed of their own childhood because they had been molested or suffered abuse. "Chesters" or "chomos" preyed on children on the outside; in prison the roles were reversed and the inmates preyed on the chesters. Even criminals needed someone to despise.

When new inmates first joined a prison gang they were expected to work and follow orders without question. They were schooled in all the proper tactics of prison warfare. Whatever they owned they had to share with the gang, and every inmate in the gang had to pay "taxes," about 20 percent. Most gang members were expected to be polite, maintain good hygiene, and be respectful, because respect brought better communication. The Mexican gangs seemed to earn everyone's respect, even the officers', mostly because the officers just wanted to be left alone; if a gang could police themselves, the officers were less likely to get involved.

Being ordered to kill your cellmate and spend the next two years in isolation was an honor. If an inmate was sent on a mission to kill a "rat," and succeeded, he was rewarded with a higher rank and greater respect. Then he could pass on his knowledge to new recruits. He could teach them how to write in code and hide contraband. Inmates obtained old languages through textbooks in the prison library, or had someone from the outside mail it in. The older the language, the harder it was for officers to crack the codes.

After years of taking shit from everyone in the gang, it might finally be time to order some hits on his enemies.

He might want to start by ordering hits on the same guys who'd brought him into the gang, just to show them that nobody owned him. Maybe he hated someone on the yard, or maybe someone on the streets stopped sending him money. Maybe someone looked at him funny in the chow hall, or he didn't like the way another inmate ate his food at breakfast. It didn't matter, because he had a couple of "torpedoes," hit men, at his disposal, ready and willing to kill for him.

If the other homies didn't agree with his hits, he could change the rules and do it anyway. Then maybe he became a leader who declared war on rival gangs and made alliances to promote stronger unity.

He had to be careful, though, because his captains could take him out of power at any time; best not to get too big of an ego. Putting a hit on someone just so he could have his car when he got out in five to ten years was probably a bad idea. There was no job security in the gang world.

The gang hit lists were a mile long and never expired. They didn't want inmates to even think about going legit, because that would poison the minds of the youngsters working their way up the ladder. Nobody liked change in prison when it didn't benefit them.

It was a wonder how the inmates were able to communicate so precisely with one another while being confined in Adseg. Because the inmates didn't have access to phones, e-mail, or fax machines, messages were passed by courier. Messages, called "kites," were written down in a tiny hand and passed off to other inmates. Kites were delivered in person by inmates going to visits, court, or transferring to another prison. Prison buses ran daily and inmates were transferring constantly. The notes were taken anywhere that inmates were traveling. One message might be sent by three different inmates to make sure it arrived. It might take two weeks to get there, but it got there.

Secret messages didn't even need to be written in ink; urine worked too. It was invisible on paper until the inmate held it to a heat source. Messages could also be hidden in inmate drawings, or in legal mail with a fake letterhead, mailed out to P.O. boxes.

Their operation aroused less suspicion if they lived someplace rural, like Idaho. If an inmate got a phone call, he could contact his girl on the outside and she could set up a three-way conversation with a second inmate at another prison. The amazing part was that all that activity was being conducted under the roof of a maximum-security prison.

Rascal and Shotgun were both nineteen, serving five years for burglary. They were both from the San Gabriel Valley. Boxer was thirty-two and had a tattoo of a black hand on his chest. He loved to greet me on the yard with, "Hey, asshole face!" and in return I would reply, "Hey there, ya bastard."

Termite was twenty-one, from Fontana, California. He liked to make pruno and hide it in the toilet. They were just doing what they had to do to survive. There aren't too many things in life that people throw themselves completely into, expecting nothing but death in return. But they truly believed in what they were fighting for. I couldn't fault them for that. The inmates considered themselves heroes. Nothing was going to get in their way.

The prison gangs operated on fear and intimidation. For them it was about money, and the way to get money was to control the prison yards. Inmate currency was the trust accounts—inmate bank accounts. The inmate had someone from the outside, a family member, put money on his books and then he could buy whatever he needed in prison. A high-ranking gang leader sitting in prison might bring in $80,000 a year, tax-free.

The hits on the Adseg Yard were planned and coordinated. If an inmate had fallen asleep or failed to pass on a message, he would be "chin checked" by one of his homies on the yard. This was a fight with fists, and the inmates would fight until the yard gunner shot the block gun at them, while the rest of the prisoners on the yard got out of the way and watched the action. To stop fighting before the block gun was fired meant the inmate was weak and unworthy of being on the yard with the other homies. It was up to the leader, the "shot caller," the inmate with "the keys," to decide the inmate's fate later on.

A "sticking," or stabbing, on the Adseg Yard might take months for the inmates to execute, because everything had to be talked over and planned out.

Inmate Gabriel went before the prison committee. Gabriel had been stabbed on the mainline when the other inmates found out he was a child molester doing twelve years for attacking his six-year-old daughter. Inmate Gabriel was short and scrawny. On the streets he enjoyed drinking tequila and beating his wife. He survived the stabbing and asked to go on the yard in Adseg. The other Mexican inmates had assured him that he'd be safe. Inmate Gabriel refused to be placed in protective custody, and the classification committee was forced to release him to the exercise yard. By law, Gabriel was allowed outside yard time three days a week.

Two weeks went by and Inmate Gabriel settled in. One morning he was talking to his newfound friends on the yard. Everything seemed normal. His best buddy was Inmate Robles with whom he shared a cell. A few homies were playing basketball while others sat down and enjoyed the sunshine. One hit a handball over the yard wall and called to the nearest officer to retrieve it. Officer Gibbs jogged around the corner. The yard gunner, Officer Timmons, was above, sleeping. Inmate Robles took out a small piece of sharpened metal and stabbed Inmate Gabriel repeatedly in the neck. Gabriel didn't have time to react. He remained quiet, not wanting to appear like a coward for screaming. The best he could do was stagger away. Inmate Robles tossed the shank in the outside yard toilet and flushed it down the rusty pipes. Then he jumped in the yard shower and washed off all the blood and evidence. Officer Gibbs returned just in time to find Inmate Gabriel collapsed on the ground in a pool of blood.

Officer Gibbs hit his alarm, waking up the yard gunner. Gabriel survived, but finally understood he was a marked man on the mainline, and could never return to the gang again. Inmate Robles did a year more in Adseg and was released to the mainline. The overworked District Attorney didn't bother to press any charges; Inmate Robles was already serving life for homicide.

Attention Staff:
Effective immediately, fresh fruit will be removed from
the box lunches. This is to reduce violence at the prison.
Fruit is used to make prison wine, known as pruno.

One of the bad things about being a new officer was that I always had to work the holidays. I didn't mind paying my dues, but it seemed veteran officers always called in sick on holidays or the days of big sporting events, like professional boxing.

On New Year's Eve I got held over just as I pulled up my car to the main gate to leave. Sergeant Arnold was holding up a line of cars, checking officers' seniority numbers.

"What's your number?" demanded Sergeant Arnold.

"I'm not too sure."

"Well, what the fuck do you think it is?"

"680 or so."

The seniority numbers for officers changed constantly. There were 725 officers at the prison, and I was number 680.

"That's not a number, that's a fucking ZIP code. Pull your car around and go back inside. I'm holding your ass over. Happy New Year, honky!"

"Where am I working?"

"It ain't my job to tell you where to go. Call the watch office."

Sergeant Arnold had a habit of ordering officers over and then calling their homes to seduce their wives. Arnold knew he had eight hours to spend at an officer's home while they were working overtime. It was another reason I did not give the prison my home phone number.

I was ordered to work Yard Rover, which meant doing alarm checks for the buildings and picking up count slips. I used the prison pay phone to call home, but no one answered.

Getting held over made me realize why the divorce rate for officers was so high. Spouses didn't understand holdovers; many suspected their spouses were out cheating. Many of them were right.

I could see across the yard that there was activity in front of the Adseg building. When I got on the yard I spotted Officer Felix in front of the building, eating a turkey sandwich. There were cardboard boxes full of sandwiches and sodas.

"What's going on?"

"The Mexicans boarded up their cells," said Felix.

"Boarding up" meant the inmates covered their cell doors with blankets so officers couldn't see inside the cells for count.

There were a dozen officers in full riot gear getting briefed by Sergeant Pollard.

"What did they do that for?"

"They've got nothing better to do."

"Happy New Year."

"You got that right," said Felix, taking another bite of his sandwich.

The Mexican inmates had flooded the tiers by shoving towels in their toilets until the water overflowed. They shredded paper so the drains on the tiers would get clogged and the water wouldn't have any place to go but out the building doors; there was only one four-inch drain on each tier. Then they sealed the sides of their cell doors so water would not leak out, and after that they released the water all at once, like a giant tidal wave. The building's water supply had to be turned off at the main valve, and soon all the inmates were screaming that they were dying from dehydration.

"Nothing matters to the inmates if they can prove that they're tough guys," said Felix, unwrapping another sandwich.

Since the inmates had refused to come out of their cells, chemical agents were used to force them out. The extraction teams were pulling out the inmates and putting them on the Adseg Yard to decontaminate them from the chemicals. When I went inside the cellblock, it was covered in a thick fog of chemical agents. Dust from the fire extinguishers coated the ceiling lights like a winter frost. More than forty cells had their doors covered from the inside with blankets.

I grabbed a gas mask and put it on. The chemical agents hit me hard even though I was wearing the mask. I didn't remember the smell of the gas until it started to burn my nose and travel into my brain, like a worm feeding on my flesh.

The inmates were lighting fires in their cells, throwing the burning pieces of debris out from under the door or out the sides. It was easy for inmates to start a fire, just with lint from a sock. The moment one fire was put out, another one would erupt on the opposite side of the tier.

"No one ever thinks a concrete structure can burn until the inmates show you how it's done," said Felix.

Paint on the walls and wax on the floors spread fire like gasoline. The ceiling was high, but it was covered in a heavy layer of asbestos that burned easily. The Plexiglas on the doors melted and the heat cracked the concrete floors. The cellblocks weren't going to crumble, but enough damage could be done by the inmates to render them uninhabitable for a few days. It was something for the inmates to brag about, because the officers still had to clean up the mess.

"Clean that shit up, bitch!" the inmates yelled as the officers scrambled to clean the tiers.

Prisons were built with the idea of housing people who quietly did their time, not criminals who continued to wreak havoc. The prison was considered new, but the cell walls leaked when it rained, and the desert winds deteriorated the buildings.

The Mexicans had a no-standing policy: no homie could walk out after boarding up; he had to be dragged out by the extraction teams. Inmate Ramos had been in prison for 20 years. He was paroling first thing the next morning, but he was one of the homies and he had to ride with the others. So the officers extracted him and dragged him out to the Adseg Yard with the others for boarding up.

I was handed a red fire extinguisher. Within seconds I saw a fire erupt on the upper tier and I raced up to put it out. Officer Felix was there struggling to get a blanket out through a cell-door food port. He abandoned his efforts and joined me. It was difficult to communicate with the gas masks on; mine made my head feel like it was in a vise.

"Put the fire out first in the cell and then out on the tier, like this!" said Felix, shoving the fire extinguisher nozzle against the door and spraying the inside of the cell.

"How are the inmates going to breathe?" I shouted.

"That's a medical issue, dawg, not a fire issue!" said Felix.

"But they haven't done anything to me!"

"It's New Year's! They didn't fuck up your night?"

"Sure they did, but I'm getting paid for it!"

Felix stuck the nozzle of the fire extinguisher under the door and gave it a burst. The inmates inside the cell coughed and sputtered. I thought for sure it would kill them, but it only angered them, like poking a stick at a caged animal.

"Hell, this is fun," said Felix. "Where else can you flock someone like a Christmas tree?"

"No thanks."

"The brass are at home," Felix assured me.

Felix sprayed another cell, but this time the inmates inside were ready: they threw a cup of urine, splashing my face. Some got inside the gas mask, soaking my head and neck.

"All right," I yelled, "it's payback time!"

"Atta boy!" cheered Felix.

I was trying to help the inmates, and they'd acted like I'd just declared World War III on them. I learned that night to never try to help an inmate, under any circumstance; inmates were always too self-absorbed to realize you were looking out for them.

Getting gassed reminded me of a mailman going to someone's front door and getting shit thrown at him just as he opened the mail slot. The other inmates in the unit were overjoyed to see that an officer had been gassed by an inmate.

"I hope you get AIDS and die, pig!" shouted an inmate. "Shit boy! Shit boy! Golden showers from my dick, bee-otch!"

I felt humiliated but there was nothing I could do to retaliate. The cell door was locked.

I rushed downstairs to the bathroom and washed off my clothing. I smelled urine, but God only knew whatever else the inmate had mixed in the cup.

Felix advised me to get over to the infirmary and file a medical report. It was a long walk down the roadway to the infirmary. I kept playing the incident back over in my head.

At the infirmary I had to hand over my uniform so that it could be used for evidence, in case the District Attorney decided to prosecute the inmate for battery.

"The uniform needs to be sent to a lab to determine if bodily fluids have been used during the assault," said a nurse.

"Can't you just look in his medical file to see if he has AIDS?"

"Oh, no."

"Why not?"

"Officers need a court order to check an inmate's medical file. The inmates have privacy rights. You should keep an extra uniform in the trunk of your car, because it'll happen again. That's what I do."

I was given blue paper shorts like they gave the inmates, and was waiting for the doctor to come check me out when suddenly the infirmary alarm sounded. Officers ran past me. While I stood awkwardly in the hallway wondering what was going on, Sergeant Arnold rushed by and stopped. He didn't recognize me.

"Get down, dumb fuck!" ordered Arnold. "There's an alarm going off!"

"I'm not an inmate, I'm an officer."

"You're a fucking liar! Now get down!" Arnold demanded.

Before I could say another word, Arnold shoved me into one of the cells and locked the door. He took off down the hallway. I shouted for him to open the door. I kicked and pounded on it but no one heard me.

"Just throw some shit out the door," shouted an inmate from the cell next to me. "That always gets their attention."

11

SHOWER SHARK

Attention Staff:
The prison is proud to announce plans for the Prison Puppies Program. The State has secured funding to begin building dog kennels. Each inmate will be assigned his own puppy that he will train and live with in is cell. Many officers have complained about the inmates training the animals to attack officers. Please direct all questions and concerns to your union reps.

was in the medical cell for an hour before Nurse Tripodi walked by and recognized me. The next day I was back at work in Adseg. In the afternoon I was on the top tier serving chow with the other officers when Sergeant Pollard walked by with an announcement.

"See you guys later," Pollard called out. "I quit."

"Where you going?" asked Felix.

"I'm turning in my stripes. Fuck this place," said Pollard.

Pollard picked up a chair and threw it across the dayroom then stormed out of the building. Pollard had quit six times in the past two years. He went on paid leave, claiming stress. Later, when he tried to come back as a sergeant, the administration wouldn't let him. They took away his sergeant stripes, claiming he was mentally unstable. Pollard tried to sue the prison for discrimination; he said they were racist against white officers. He didn't win.

I saw Pollard at an off-duty party that weekend. I hated going to off-duty parties but I did it to gain the trust of the officers. Officer Gibbs was getting married for the third time, and having a bachelor party. In true prison fashion he hired two female strippers to give him lap dances. Pollard was crying on the kitchen floor when I arrived. He was upset the prison had refused to re-instate him as sergeant.

"I should have made sergeant!" Pollard cried.

Pollard's third wife of three weeks approached me, smelling of tequila. Her name was Julie and she was an officer well-known for having slept with half of the officers. The other officers referred to her as "Scary Larry" because she was both ugly and looked like a man.

"My husband is a pussy," she slurred. "I want to fuck you right now."

"I'm very flattered, but I'm gonna have to pass."

"So, you'll take a rain check?"

"No. I'm gonna have to pass all together."

She fell to the floor and started snoring. Pollard crawled over to his wife and hugged her.

Even though I didn't like Pollard, I felt sorry for him. Pollard was no different than a lot of other prison guards.

Attention Staff:

Inmates have been complaining that officers have been using an excessive amount of pepper spray during incidents. Please wait 2–3 seconds before and after deploying bursts of chemical agents.

The next day I was sent to Bravo One Control. The comfort zone from Adseg was gone, replaced with the same anxiety I had come to know from my very first day. During my first five minutes in Bravo One Control, Inmate Forbes started kicking his cell door and shouting for me, like it was an emergency. When an inmate kicked his door, it resonated throughout the housing unit like a clap of thunder. There was no way to ignore it.

"I want my motherfucking pizza, tower!" Inmate Forbes screamed.

I got on the intercom and hollered back at him.

"What pizza?"

"You know what pizza, bitch! I want my fucking pizza, bitch!"

"I want my shoes!" I yelled. "Give me my shoes!"

"What the fuck are you talking about?"

"When you give me my shoes, I'll give you your pizza!"

"I'm not an idiot. I know my rights, you fucking shower shark!" The inmates liked to refer to the tower officer as "shower shark" because he had a direct view of the inmate showers.

"Then fight for your rights!"

I proceeded to ignore Inmate Forbes, figuring he was insane. After awhile he stopped kicking the door; I thought I had resolved the problem. To my amazement a food cart arrived at Inmate Forbes' cell door with an extra-large pizza. Officer Gibbs motioned for me to open the door. I opened the door and Inmate Forbes grabbed the pizza box and held it up.

"Told you I'd get my pizza, bitch!"

Sergeant Arnold had ordered pizzas for the inmates because there had been no murders that month on the yard.

Attention Staff:
The purpose of this memo is to announce the creation of the Honor Program. This program is designed for inmates who want to be free from violence, illegal drugs, and disruptive behavior. The Honor Program is defined as a voluntary context in which inmates commit themselves to respect and excellence.

The inmates knew that the floor officers were the ones to talk to because the officer in the tower had no control over what went on below; but to irritate the tower, the inmates asked meaningless questions. I learned to give them back meaningless answers.

"Hey, tower, what time is it?" an inmate would ask.

"What time do you want it to be?"

"Hey, tower, what tier has yard today?"

"The fifty-fifth tier."

"Tower, turn on my motherfucking air!"

"Have your cellie blow in your ear."

"Tower, you got any soap?"

"Damn, I just used it to shower."

"Tower, call Charlie Yard and see where my property is!"

"You call them."

"Tower, can you open cell 222 so I can get some soups?"

"The door is broken."

"Tower, can you let out 117 so he can cut my hair?"

"Your hair looks fine."

"Tower, I need my worker shower."

"No, you smell fantastic."

"Tower, what's for chow?"

"State food."

The sooner I could establish that I wasn't there to help the inmates, the better; that way the inmates would stop asking questions. If an inmate's cell was searched, it was the fault of the first officer the inmate saw, which was me. The officers tried to search the cells when the inmates weren't in the housing blocks, then leave before the inmate returned, to avoid confrontation. This was usually done at chow time. The only certainty about running a housing unit was getting gamed by the inmates—no matter how many years I had on the job, no matter how closely I paid attention. It was up to a good officer to decide what was worth getting gamed over and what wasn't. The inmates weren't going to respect an officer if he let them walk all over him.

"Why the fuck did you hit my house, tower?" Inmate Forbes demanded.

"How could I go into your cell? I'm up here."

"Well, you opened the door and let the officers in!"

"That's my job."

"Why didn't you stop them? Who was it? I want their names! I'll have their badges!"

The inmates could never answer a question. They had poor communication skills. They were so programmed to defend themselves that they would answer a question with a question. When an inmate would come to the back door of the housing unit and ask to come inside, I'd ask him his name and cell number. I didn't want to let an inmate from a different cellblock inside the wrong unit; inmates tried daily to gain access to areas of the prison where they were not permitted. It seemed harmless, but inmates were always trying to get into restricted areas in order to commit crimes.

"Where do you live?" I asked Inmate Ferrara as he tried to get inside. Inmate Ferrara was twenty-six and from Artesia, California. He was serving six years for armed robbery.

"Where do I live?" he responded.

"Yes, where do you live?"

"I'm a yard-crew worker."

"I asked you where you lived."

"I work on the yard. Can I get a shower?"

Every inmate worker got a shower when coming back into the unit. Still, the inmates were convinced that they were going to get passed over even though they'd had the same schedule for the last five years.

"Where do you live?"

"I live in a cell."

"In what cell?"

"I'm a worker. Can I get a shower? Let me in. I'm coming back from work."

Inmates would stay out on the yard after work or school and play with their friends instead of going back to their cells. I would see them playing basketball or volleyball on the yard, but then they would lie and say they had just gotten off work a minute ago. Because there were only six showers for 200 inmates, it made it nearly impossible to accommodate everyone without a schedule.

"Listen, all I want to know is what cell you're in."

"Are you calling me a child molester? I'm telling the captain you called me a child molester!"

There were days I felt like pulling the trigger. They never knew how lucky they were.

Attention Staff:
Several officers were arrested this past weekend in a prostitution sting by the Sheriff's Department. The officers were stopped along State Highway and their vehicles were impounded. Officers are reminded to be professional on and off duty.

The cell doors on Bravo Yard weren't built for Level Four inmates; the yard was supposed to be for Level Three. The prison was all Level Four, a maximum-security prison. On the Level Four yards, the doors could be opened and closed only by the Tower Officer; but on a Level Three yard, the doors could be opened only by the control booth officer. It was up to the inmates to close the doors when it was time to lock up, but some of the inmates didn't always feel like doing it. The inmates knew that the only way the control officer could tell whether the doors were closed was if the red light on the control panel lit up. Some of the inmates had learned to watch the control officer and shut the door in just such a way that, from the control booth, it appeared to be locked—but wasn't.

Even after having the floor officer check the cell doors, I might find inmates opening their doors and wandering the tiers, trying to get on the phones after the floor officer had left the building.

"Can I get a phone call?" Inmate Ortiz asked, suddenly appearing from nowhere. Two years was added onto his sentence for his escape and he was sent back to the yard.

"No."

"Then can I get a shower?"

"No," I repeated.

"Can I go get something from the upper tier?"

"No."

"Why you gotta be working with feelings, C.O.?"

"What part of 'no' do you not understand?"

"Fuck you!"

The inmates spent each day goofing off, just like kids on a playground. An inmate would be ironing his shirt and another inmate would sneak up from behind and pull down his pants. If that didn't get laughs, then he would poke him in the ear with his finger; that usually had the other inmates roaring.

The inmates were on "prison time"; one minute to them was like an hour to a normal person. That's why the shower program was so chaotic: the inmates never took into consideration that there were other inmates waiting to use the shower before and after them. They had no patience. They wanted to jump in the shower the moment they got inside the housing unit. The same thing happened when they signed up for the phones. They just assumed that officers would tell them what time to get on the phone. It didn't matter where they were in the prison. They would sign up for a two o'clock phone call knowing they'd be at school, and then they'd ask five hours later why they didn't get to use the phone.

Attention Staff:
The budget crisis has placed hardships on all of us. While it is tempting to put the blame on one side or the other, no one is at fault. The union is here to help all of us in these troubled times. Now is the time to demonstrate to the people that we are professionals. It is time to show the public that we will carry out the duty of the state within the rules that govern our jobs.

The most difficult movement on the yard was at third watch shift change, 2:00 p.m., because all the inmates would be coming back from their various programs. I arrived early each shift to catch up on the events of the day, but it never failed that the control officer on second watch, Officer Gibbs, would leave without saying anything. Officer Gibbs could dish it out, but he sure couldn't take it. Most of the other officers didn't like him because he was such a crybaby. He loved video games, and brought his Nintendo Game Boy with him every day. Gibbs was now single, living in a Motel 6. Second watch positions were almost always occupied by veteran officers with seniority.

"Nothing much happened today, dawg," said Gibbs. "Everything's good."

The control booth seemed to give officers temporary amnesia after eight hours. Officers rarely remembered to tell others anything. Second watch officers knew there was information to pass on, but they were more focused on making it out the gate without getting held over. There might be inmates in the showers who got in a fight earlier that day, or an inmate who needed to move to another building. The inmates weren't going to tell you they got fired from their jobs or weren't supposed to be out of their cells; that was the officer's job.

After Officer Gibbs left, I would be stuck for the next fifteen minutes running around passing out equipment to the yard staff, answering the phone, or taking inventory of the control booth equipment to make sure nothing was missing. It was a miracle I was able to account for all the building equipment and keep track of which officer had what. There were items on the weapons log that no longer existed, but were checked off because officers just signed the log without reading it.

All the equipment for the Yard was kept in Building One. The phone always took up time because strangers called constantly, asking for officers I'd never heard of. It never failed that the person on the other end would not identify him or herself, so I never knew who was hassling me for some mindless information. I was, however, always careful not to be rude because I never knew if the person on the other end might be the warden.

"Who's this?" a caller would ask.

"The control officer."

"Where is Lopez?"

"The inmate or the officer?"

"Where's Lopez at?"

"I don't know who that is."

"Fuck you, liar!"

For some reason everyone assumed the control booth officer knew everything, like the phone operator. The same concept applied when the floor officers got the inmate count wrong. The supervisors always called the control officer to ask why the floor count was bad, but I couldn't ask the floor staff directly why they had a bad count, because they would get upset and accuse me of trying to boss them around. I didn't know what was going on in the cells unless the floor staff stopped to tell me. The supervisors just wanted a voice to yell at.

"It seems that every time I call you on the phone you have an attitude," said Sergeant Arnold. "It seems you harbor personal feelings against me."

"No, sir," I said biting my tongue. "I'm trying to be part of the solution, not the problem. I'm just trying to do my job."

The equipment shadow board had numbers for the keys, but if an officer lost a pair of handcuffs or a baton, there were no corresponding numbers to indicate that they belonged to the building. I had more than a hundred pieces of equipment to be responsible for every day.

It was always important to at least count the ammunition in case the control booth officer from the previous shift lost a round. An officer could get away with missing equipment, but losing a round of ammunition caused panic with administration. No one wanted the inmates to make a "zip gun" and kill an officer.

The weapons log that needed to be filled out every shift looked like a decades-old crossword puzzle. Sergeant Arnold would come in one day and erase certain equipment from the log, then replace it the next week without telling anyone. I would try to explain to second watch staff that they couldn't leave, because I was responsible for the equipment. But also, I didn't want to be a snitch and tell the supervisor. Because I was new, they would just shrug.

I had to track down officers and beg them to turn in their equipment. The responsibility didn't fall on the floor cops, so they didn't care about looking out for me. Every day I would have to ask the floor staff if they had any equipment. It never failed that an officer left the housing unit with equipment in his jacket pocket or lunch bag. This was never done deliberately; officers were just lazy and careless.

Then the hunt was on for the officer before he got to the pedestrian gate. Once I'd manage to get hold of the officer, it was always the same argument.

"You've got the alarm," I would say on the phone.

"No, I don't."

"Yes, you do. I wouldn't be calling you if you didn't."

"No, dawg, it's somewhere up there. Just keep looking."

"I *have* been looking, and now it's time for you to bring it back."

Rather than take a moment to double check, the officers would spend their time arguing with me, because staff was never wrong.

"You don't have to talk to me like I'm a child," they'd whine.

"Actually, I *do*, because you're not being responsible."

I made enemies on Bravo Yard because I attempted to do my job the right way. I constantly met with resistance from officers who didn't want to work, so I finally stopped tracking them down. I would just note in the log book that the equipment was missing, and contact Sergeant Arnold—who, just like Officer Gibbs, simply did not give a shit. It took me years to realize I was the only one concerned about missing equipment.

Attention Staff:
A catastrophic time bank has been formed for Officer Pollard. Officer Pollard is seeking donations for breast augmentation surgery. Officers wishing to donate to

Officer Pollard's time bank may donate holiday and vacation time, but not sick time.

There were four phones in each housing unit. The inmates were allowed fifteen minutes for each call. The phone was on a timer and would alert the caller when there were two minutes remaining. Then the connection would shut off automatically. It was done this way so inmates couldn't blame the control booth officer for turning off the phone in the middle of their conversations, but they did anyway. The control booth officer could listen to both ends of the conversation; there was a speakerphone next to the control panel.

They were always the same conversations.

"Hey, Mom. I need, like, forty dollars."

"What for? I just sent you a hundred last week."

"Oh, well, we're getting some burritos," the inmate lied. "And they're like ten bucks each and I wanted to get like five for my buddies. They don't have no money."

Attention Staff:
We are pleased to announce the new and improved breast-feeding station for officers located next to the barbershop in the Administration Building. Female officers may now breast-feed in the comfort of the new breast-feeding station.

The floor staff left the building to run chow around three o'clock. Floor officers were assigned to watch the inmates inside the chow hall during dinner; they didn't come back until six o'clock. That left three hours where I was alone. The only way I could properly run the building was by applying a type of chaos theory: the inmates could do whatever they wanted within reason until the floor officers came back; then the inmates had to "lock up"—go back into their cells. This way, it looked like I had the building under control for the entire duration. I was giving the inmates something for their time.

At chow time I would be called on the phone from an officer at the chow hall to release the building. I would open a third of the cell doors and wait for the inmates to exit, then close the cell doors. This took time because the inmates always forgot something and had to go back in their cells for it—usually, their state ID cards, spoons, or cups. Inmates always had to show their state ID cards at chow time. Two different officers would come into the building and direct the inmates out of the housing unit. The inmates were issued one plastic spoon and cup; they cleaned them in their own sinks.

The inmates never moved as fast as I wanted them to. They were on "state time." I always announced "state minutes" as a preface to anything with a time frame, so that the inmates wouldn't get anxious. "State time" meant that it would get done when it got done. The inmates always expected the prison to come through with its side of the bargain to take care of them on time. While most of the inmates walked to the chow hall, others stayed behind to take showers or watch TV in the day room.

"Ten state minutes to chow! Ten state minutes!" I'd call over the intercom.

To keep track of the inmates, there were supposed to be "bed cards," three-by-five-inch cards with information and a photo of each inmate posted in the control booth. I had none. The prison hadn't printed them in years.

The cell doors were supposed to have each inmate's name and number posted but every time a new door tag went up, an inmate would rip it down. Door tags were put up by the inmate porters; the floor officers weren't going to waste their time if they could get an inmate porter to do it.

I used word association to remember inmates' names, and wrote down each cell number along with a certain funny characteristic to remember its inmate. Inmate Perez had a pony tail. Inmate Carter wore Coke-bottle glasses. Inmate Richter had his name tattooed across his forehead.

I tried to remember where the inmates lived, so I could lock them up faster. Some inmates were easy to identify, but it would take me weeks to figure out others; it didn't help that, for the most part, they all dressed in prison blues. To add to my confusion, Inmates Gomez and Gomez were identical twins. Inmates Ford and Smith were father and son, and strongly resembled one another.

It actually helped me when the inmates got their hands on name-brand clothing smuggled inside. The inmates also altered their state clothing by sewing home-made insignias mimicking Nike or Puma to their shirts, pants, and hats.

There was no emergency radio in the control booth, so I was limited to calling officers on the phone in case of an emergency—if I was lucky enough to know their extension. Most of the time I just shouted down to the officers and hoped they could hear me.

The control booth telephone was one step up from an antique rotary phone. It crackled constantly with an ear-numbing static. I found an old copy of the prison directory and called the phone technician time and time again. His name was Leo. He was in his fifties, weighed 400 pounds, and loved to wear Hawaiian shirts. He always had food in his hands.

"I need the phone fixed in Bravo One Control, please."

"Your phone work fine, brah. I hear you good," said Leo.

"No, it's broken."

"No, it work good. Can hear just fine, bro!"

"Can you come and look at it anyway?"

"Put in a work order, brah. I get to it in a few weeks."

The phone never got fixed. The same held true for the plumbers and the electricians; no one ever saw them around the prison unless it was an administrative emergency. They were paid overtime after 5:00 p.m.; officers used inmate plumbers because they were more accessible and would work after five. I got used to having problems with maintenance, so I brought in Liquid Drano when the sink got clogged and a plunger when the toilets overflowed.

The control booth also lacked basic supplies, like paper, staples, paperclips, Scotch tape, toilet paper, and paper towels. I bought my own supplies after realizing that no one was going to deliver them, even though I had put in repeated requests to the warehouse. I had to keep the supplies in my locker because anything left out in the control booths would be stolen by other officers.

Written on the wall of the control booth bathroom was a reminder from officers who had held the position prior to me: *"DO NOT GIVE AWAY ANY SUPPLIES FROM THIS CONTROL BOOTH TO INMATES ON THE FLOOR. IT IS HARD ENOUGH TO GET SUPPLIES!"*

I finally found out why I never got any supplies. One day I was throwing away "hot trash" at the back of the prison. "Hot trash" was trash that could not be thrown away inside the prison because it might be made into a weapon. Officers carried hot trash outside the prison and placed it in designated trash bins. When I threw away my bag of trash, I looked inside the bin; it was full of brand-new, neatly wrapped office supplies. Someone who worked in the prison warehouse hid them there in order to take them home.

Attention Staff:
While no one is happy about a reduction in the corrections budget, the administration has developed a proposal that is smart on crime, cuts inmate population, and saves taxpayer dollars. It is our hope that this reasonable package will allow our budget-cut target to not effect the early release of inmates.

In the summer months officers had to deal with rolling electrical blackouts. The electric companies who figured out they could make millions by shutting down the power grids for several hours daily yet still charged customers. It seemed no one in administration thought it was a good idea to let the officers know when a blackout was going to occur. Come six o'clock, they were sitting down to dinner at home with their families; when the lights went out and we were on the floor, the only thing we could do was pray for a miracle. The inmates would kill us simply because there were no witnesses.

Officer Haggerty, the ex-stripper was on the tier minutes after the last inmate had locked up for count when the power went out suddenly. When the power went out, the cellblock air conditioner grounded to a screeching halt, followed by dead silence. Then the inmates threw themselves against their cell doors trying to get at her.

"I can smell you, bitch!" yelled an inmate.

"Oh, my God!" screamed Haggerty.

"Are you okay?" I shouted frantically into the abyss.

"She's okay with my dick in her ass!" yelled another inmate.

"Are you okay?" I repeated. "Tell me you're all right!"

Silence.

I didn't know whether any of the inmates had managed to get out of their cells. I grabbed the rifle and was about to fire blindly into the darkness. I racked a round into the chamber. Suddenly, the lights flickered back on. I could just barely make out Officer Haggerty, huddled in the corner next to the utility closet with her hands over her face. When the lights returned to full strength, the inmates saw me with the rifle out the window and Officer Haggerty crying in the corner. They let off a round of cheers. Officer Haggerty quit that night.

After the six o'clock count, the inmate kitchen workers would wander back with bags full of food leftover from the chow hall. Officer Timmons was the kitchen officer. Timmons had been bitten twice on the yard by the same gopher; he was certain if he caught the gopher it would make a perfect pet for his daughter. The other officers on the yard had bets that Timmons was going to die from gopher rabies. Timmons let the inmates steal all the food they wanted. Food theft was rampant and lunches were always missing in every housing unit.

It didn't take a genius to figure out that if you had 1,000 inmates on a yard, you needed 1,100 lunches, because certain inmates and officers were going to take them. Officers didn't want to be bothered passing out lunches, so they always had the inmates do it. There was no stopping the theft of state food, because officers didn't want to have to work to enforce the rules. This was always a topic of discussion for the inmates. The kitchen workers liked to gripe to me after work.

"Man, the food is going to be thrown out anyway. Why not give it to the inmates?"

"Because it's stealing," I'd say.

"Well, the way I see it, they don't pay us enough to work in the kitchen. The extra food is an incentive."

"When you become warden, you can change the rules."

"But we're starvin' up in this joint!"

Inmate workers were allowed to eat all day, but always complained they were starving. The inmate kitchen workers took the food back to their units and sold it for a profit. Because the kitchen officer refused to search the inmates, I refused to let the inmates back in the building. I would call the yard gunner to request officers to report to the building to search the culinary workers, but no officers would show up. So, I'd be left with ten inmates screaming to take their worker showers, while at the same time I had a dayroom full of inmates roaming around asking why I wasn't letting the culinary workers in the building.

Sergeant Arnold called, "Why are the inmate culinary workers standing outside the building?"

"Because they haven't been searched yet."

"Can't you handle the inmates in your building? How hard is it to press a button?"

It was a favorite phrase for most supervisors.

The only thing that I could use against the inmates when they didn't "program" was the two TVs in the day room. Most of the inmates had a television in their cells, but the dayroom TVs were like a life-support system for those who didn't. Television was everyone's hobby. It was something to talk about, and the best babysitter the prison had. Inmates scheduled their lives around televised sports and reality shows. Those inmates with TVs locked up quicker so that they could go watch *Monday Night Football* or March Madness basketball. Officers loved sports too, and were always eager to lock up the inmates quicker if there was a game to watch. A lot of gambling on sports went on inside the prison walls.

The housing unit had its share of problems. Most inmate stabbings came to my attention when the inmate wandered in a daze past the podium with blood gushing from his side. The victim never wanted to identify the attacker, because he wasn't considered a man if he snitched.

Inmates "handled business" by beating up an enemy and tossing him in the shower. Then someone would yell, "Man down in the shower!"

This would alert the building staff, but the victim would still insist he slipped in the shower and had no idea where those stab wounds came from.

If everything went smoothly I could shut down the dayroom at 9:00 p.m., but it would take another half-hour to get the inmates back in their cells with the doors properly closed. Nighttime lock-up was worse than yard recall because the inmates needed to be counted by 9:30; this was the final count for third watch. They weren't getting out of their cells until the morning, so the inmates took their time locking up. Dayroom was from 7:00 p.m. to 9:00 p.m.—a hundred inmates running loose for two hours on the cellblock floor. It was impossible to watch them all.

The inmates had all evening to run errands, but every night they chose to jump in the shower or get on the phone when nine o'clock rolled around. The inmates wanted to pass items to one another, and wanted me to open the cell doors so they could get their business done. The inmates could never handle their business on their own time; it always had to conflict with the officers trying to do their jobs. The inmates would hold items up to the doors, pleading with me to open them just enough so they could pass something to another inmate. Helping inmates pass items from one cell to another was prohibited—an officer might be passing along a weapon or drugs without knowing it.

After the inmates locked up I still had to wait for the three inmate program clerks who were busy kicking back in the office right next to Sergeant Arnold's office. The clerks were late every night, but there was nothing I could do because Sergeant Arnold gave them extra time to screw around. The inmate clerks typed all his paperwork.

The building officers were told to "shadow count" the inmate clerks; it meant the inmates were counted even though they weren't in a cell. If Central Control heard an officer say "shadow count," they acted like he was speaking Mandarin.

"There is no such thing as a shadow count at this prison," insisted Sergeant Arnold.

"Yes, sir, I know, but the inmates aren't in the building yet."

"Why not? Where are they? All inmates must be in their cells by 21:30 hours."

To call in a bad count showed that you couldn't run your housing unit.

If turning off the TVs didn't work, I had to write up the inmates, which took too much time out of my shift. I started writing reports out of pure frustration—reports for delaying count, smoking in the dayroom, out of bounds, disobeying a direct order, and threatening staff. The reports were all thrown out, due to "insufficient evidence." If the inmate clerks didn't "lose" them, Sergeant Arnold dismissed them.

All my hard work was tossed in the trash. The inmates had the last laugh because Sergeant Arnold didn't want to have to roll up any of them and send them to Adseg.

Sergeant Arnold wanted to keep the number of write-ups down on Bravo Yard so that from the outside things looked good.

The write-ups meant I was following through with what I had told the inmates I was going to do. Without the authority, I had nothing over the inmates. If there were no ramifications for their infractions, the inmates would think I was a joke.

"You didn't include the who, what, when, where, why, and how," Sergeant Arnold scoffed after tossing my report in the trash.

"Yes, I did."

"So, you stand by your report?" Arnold demanded.

"I stand by my report."

"Rewrite it and get it back to me next week."

My reports mysteriously disappeared. Nothing was ever said of them. Other reports would lose time constraints because they had to be heard in fifteen days or the inmates walked. The very system I tried to enforce turned against me and made it impossible for me to do my job correctly. There was no way to win, so I gave up.

The moment an inmate got hurt as a result of the prison's lack of security, the officers were blamed. The prison pointed fingers. What was said out loud was never put on paper. The prison was reactive, never proactive.

If Sergeant Arnold ordered me to let an inmate out and that inmate stabbed someone, then I got the blame, not the sergeant.

When I asked for memos to protect myself, I was looked at like I was a troublemaker. When I asked questions, I was deemed difficult.

In time I kept to myself when asked how things were going, because the supervisors never actually wanted to know the truth. They just wanted to hear that everything was running smoothly on their yard. The policy was, "Don't fix what works."

"After twenty years you'll be like a beaten-down dog," insisted Sergeant Arnold. "So why even start caring in the first place? The only thing certain for officers is divorce and death."

It took me years to discover that there was no point in getting worked up if an inmate didn't walk fast enough to chow or if the inmates slow-dragged it to their cells.

In December a riot erupted between black and Mexican inmates over drug debts. Dozens of the more than 300 rioters were injured. Officers were able to stop the riot after deploying chemical agents and rounds from the block guns. Bravo Yard was placed on lock-down, and the inmates' privileges were revoked until the incident was investigated.

Inmates attacked three correctional officers in August. They had conspired for months to kill officers over restricted privileges, and they might have succeeded if some of the inmates involved in the assaults hadn't strayed from the original plan. Officer Schultz suffered a fractured jaw and took a year off. Sergeant Arnold was knocked out and left for dead in a cellblock. He was back to work the next day. Officer Tadlock was stabbed repeatedly and his fingers cut off. He was medically retired.

The prison launched an investigation into the attacks, confiscating more than 70 homemade weapons from the yard. More than fifteen inmates were charged with conspiracy to commit murder. Some of the inmates involved in the conspiracy slipped through the cracks of the investigation and remained on the yard, while their associates were transferred to other prisons or paroled.

A few months later the tension eased. Life went on in the prison. The violence went in cycles. There were more calm days than there were crazy. Things became easier for me too in the control booth. The program ran smoother because I got to know the inmates. The inmates knew what to expect from me. They actually came to rely on me. On my days off the inmates missed me, because the program did not run smoothly when I was gone. Whenever a newer officer would come in for the day, the program would be turned upside down because he or she would be enforcing rules that the inmates weren't used to. The only way to run a smooth program was to be consistent.

One particular evening Officer Campos, fresh from the Academy, was on the floor. Campos had already acquired the nickname "The Angry Dwarf" from fellow officers. Campos was short, with small hands and a pencil-thin neck. He was arrogant and immature. Rather than tell the inmates on the floor to do something, Campos ordered the other officers to tell the inmates, like he was a supervisor. "Tell that inmate to put his shirt on," he demanded.

I had always tried to be polite to new officers because I knew what it was like to be the fish, and I tried to be patient.

"You tell him, he's right next to you."

"Tell that inmate to stop smoking in the dayroom," Campos demanded.

Officer Gibbs was working overtime, and leaning against the podium next to Campos. Gibbs was on a double shift and wanted a smooth overtime. Gibbs looked up at me from a magazine and grinned.

"Look, man," said Gibbs. "It's not hurting anyone, and they're leaving us alone."

"But it's illegal!" Campos cried. "They're committing a crime. It's in direct violation of prison policy."

"There's a way to do things, and walking over to that table is going to get you stabbed."

"I'm going to call the sergeant," Campos threatened.

"Shit, be my guest," Gibbs laughed.

Gibbs picked up the phone and dialed the sergeant. He handed the phone to Campos. I was shocked when Sergeant Arnold bothered to come over to the building.

Sergeant Arnold redirected Campos to sweep the yard for weapons with a metal detector for the rest of the night. Then he made him collect water samples from the prison yard. Whenever a supervisor wanted to get rid of an officer, he sent him to sweep the yard or collect water samples. It was the only time I ever agreed with Sergeant Arnold.

After one year on the job I got a generic performance evaluation from a supervisor I had never worked with or even met. I was given all "satisfactory" marks.

At first I was bitter, because I felt I was a better officer than most; but after awhile it dawned on me that even if I got an excellent evaluation I really couldn't do anything with it. Evaluations didn't dictate pay raises or promotions. We were union workers and we got raises when our contracts were renegotiated. Our union dues supported politicians who held positions on committees and boards that helped employees get raises. It was always about money.

I reflected back on my twelve months as a correctional officer and it occurred to me that I hadn't learned much. I was too scared to absorb anything. I couldn't get comfortable in my surroundings because every day was different. I needed more time to learn the job. After third watch ended, I walked to the employee parking lot with Officer Felix. It was ten-thirty at night. A sheriff's deputy was waiting for Sergeant Arnold with an orange jumpsuit. The Sheriff's Department was right next door to the prison so it was always a treat for the deputies to drive over and arrest a prison guard. It was the county laughing at the state.

Sergeant Arnold had gotten into a fight with his wife and broken her arm after she said she wanted to go out drinking with her friends instead of staying home with him. Arnold didn't have any sick days left, so he went to work with the idea that he'd take his wife to the doctor on his next day off. He didn't think she'd call the police.

Felix chuckled. "That's the third arrest this month."

12

SOAP, CLIPPERS, AND A RAZOR

Attention Staff:
The freedom to voice discontent at organized events
is a right guaranteed by the Constitution. However,
this does not permit you to do so on state time. If you
wish to voice your opinion, this needs to be done on
your own time and at your own expense. Supporting
causes at the taxpayers' expense is against the law.
Attending events in state vehicles and on state time
is prohibited.

In January an officer was stabbed to death on the tier. The department was quick to blame the officer for letting the inmate out of his cell. Administration blamed the prison for not issuing the stab-proof vests that had been sitting in the prison warehouse for the past year. The murder reinforced that officers were expendable.

A month later I was placed back in the hole. In Adseg, I developed my own program for dealing with the inmates. I didn't care if they didn't clean their cells. I didn't care if they weren't in compliance with grooming standards, or if they wrote on the walls or put up pornography. The brass didn't like the inmates "fishing," but I allowed them to fish on the tiers. The inmates were allowed only one magazine at a time, but I allowed them to have as many as they wanted; it was giving the inmates something in a world where they had very little.

It also gave me something to take away from them if the inmates didn't "program," or follow the rules. Officers weren't supposed to bargain with the inmates, but in The Hole it was the only method that worked. I didn't believe in being petty over the rules, because then there was nothing to show the inmates that I was meeting them halfway.

There was no reason to use force on the inmates when you could take away their property, visits, canteen, and yard, as well as restrict their meals. It changed the inmates' attitude when they knew an officer had leverage.

I believed in rewarding the inmates when they helped me out. Of course, there was nothing in the rulebook about rewarding inmates, but there should have been. Each inmate got a shower three times a week for fifteen minutes. The showers started after evening chow was served and the trash was picked up. No inmate ever took exactly fifteen minutes in the shower. The shower was an escape. A mini-vacation away from their cells. The inmates wanted as much time as possible out of their cells. I learned early on to ask inmates if they wanted a shower or a state item, like a pen or a book. Because these items were hard to come by and not illegal for me to give the inmates, it was a win-win. I never had one complaint from the inmates.

The prison was changing. It now had a protective custody yard to protect the inmates from other inmates. These "sensitive needs" inmates could no longer be on the mainline. Inmates were locking up themselves for protection for snitching on inmates or dropping out of the gang life. These inmates used to be called Protective Custody (PC) inmates, but the administration said that was too harsh and insensitive a label, so it was changed to Sensitive Needs. The SN were like the Witness Protection Program, but in a prison.

The same inmates who had spent years locked in The Hole were now walking around on the Sensitive Needs Yards with a Bible, saying, "I'm a Christian now, brother."

When I first got to the prison I didn't understand that the state protected the inmates from the inmates. I was shocked when Inmate Ortiz, sitting on the benches in the middle of the yard after chow, told me he wanted to go to The Hole. Ortiz was the same inmate who had escaped from the minimum yard. He bet on everything, and usually lost.

"What for?"

"Just take me to the motherfucking Hole, fish!" Ortiz screamed.

"You can't just go to The Hole. You need a reason."

"Just call the Sergeant," demanded Ortiz.

Inmate Ortiz wanted to be put in protective custody because he had bet $1,600 on a Clippers basketball game and lost. Ortiz punched me in the chest and fell to the ground, spreading his arms out. I couldn't stomp his head in because he had given up. He was no longer a threat. I handcuffed him and escorted him to the program office.

The younger inmates used to look up to the older inmates as mentors; now they just preyed on them. The old-timers were known as "convicts," but now they were known as "suckers." Inmates were coming directly from the county jails or the Youth Authority and going straight to the Sensitive Needs Yards without ever serving time on a mainline yard. A new breed of inmates were running up drug debts and then snitching on the drug dealers so they wouldn't have to pay them. Telling on each other had become the norm.

The Hole became the mental health ward. That meant that Adseg inmates who were on medication went there. It was the dumping ground for inmates that no one else could handle on psychotropic medication.

The Hole had not been designed to handle inmates serving more than a year in isolation, let alone mental patients. It required placing doctors inside the building, as well as psych techs, medical techs, and nurses. Cages were bolted to the housing unit floors in a circle so inmates could have group therapy sessions.

The inmates knew they could get sympathy from the doctors by telling them they were being beaten and abused by the guards. Since the doctors didn't understand the inmates' motives for lying, the doctors naturally thought the inmates were telling the truth. The inmates that actually needed help were ignored. They were the inmates that slept all day from taking heavy doses of medication. They never left their cells, so the doctors

assumed they were fine. The doctors were more concerned with the inmates who kicked their doors, because
such behavior was violent. Every day the inmates told
the doctors something crazy. Dr. Colby was well-known
for believing anything the inmates told her. She was in
her fifties, with long gray hair and a smoker's cough.

"The inmate in the therapeutic module needs you
to turn his pacemaker down," Dr. Colby told me one
afternoon.

"That inmate doesn't wear a pacemaker. He's only
19 years old."

"Well, why would he make that up?" she asked.

"Because he's retarded."

"Oh my God, he's retarded? Did you fill out the
proper paperwork for a handicapped inmate?"

"No, I mean he's a *ding*. He's going to tell you anything just to get a rise out of you."

"That's ridiculous," she insisted. "I'm helping my
patients. They'd never do that."

"They just did."

"Well, then, can you take my patient out of the
therapeutic module?"

"You mean the cage?"

"It's not a cage. It's a therapeutic module," Dr.
Colby insisted.

"Does the inmate know that?"

"He's not an inmate. He's a patient."

"No, he's a criminal. I can show you his file. He
murdered his parents."

"I can rehabilitate him."

A lot of people believed the inmates were innocent. My mother was one of them. Inmate Manny Chavez
showed me a picture one morning of his girlfriend standing next to a group of women. One of the women was

my smiling mother. Inmate Chavez was forty-five. He was quiet and reserved. I enjoyed talking to him and had gotten to know him rather well over time. Chavez was serving three life sentences for murder. He often complained that he wished he could spend the weekend with his girlfriend in the boneyard. He had been writing letters to Inmate Susan Little. The prison had a nursery so that female inmates could bond with their babies while incarcerated. Inmate Susan Little had stabbed her husband fifty-three times and used the battered women syndrome as her defense. It didn't work, and she was given a life sentence. My mother and her church group had been working on Little's court case for the past year, trying to get her out of prison because she had suffered abuse at the hands of her husband. My mother was taking gift baskets to the women's prison because the inmates had told her that they did not have running water or toothbrushes. The photo of my mother in the prison cell shocked me how quickly the inmates could find out information about me. My mother never thought twice about discussing my life with a total stranger in prison. No matter how much I argued with her, she couldn't see what the problem was. To my mother, Inmate Susan Little was a victim of the justice system. To my mother, I was the criminal for being a prison guard.

We had the family over for Christmas dinner. We had all sat down at the dinner table when my mother suggested we pray for the inmates.

"It's just so sad that they're all alone for the holidays," she cried.

"Well, this is my home and we're not praying for the inmates," I said.

My father-in-law agreed. "They should cut off their balls is what they should do!"

"What good would that do?" asked my dad. "That doesn't solve anything."

"You just don't get it," said my mom. "They don't even have running water."

I rolled my eyes. "They have running water, Mom."

"How do you know?" she asked.

"Because I work in a prison! Maybe you should ask me sometime before you run off and try to save the inmates."

"If I don't, then who will?"

"The state takes care of them just fine."

"You know darn well the guards beat them for no reason."

"Actually, I know damn well that's a bunch of bullshit."

My sister threw in her thoughts. "I just think it's wrong that you abuse them like that poor man in New York."

"Exactly!" shouted my mother. "The Haitian immigrant who was sodomized with a broomstick!"

"It was a plunger, Mom," added my sister.

"What does that have to do with the prison?" I demanded. "That happened in New York with police officers, not prison guards."

"Oh, you're all the same!" my mom shouted.

Attention Staff:
This week is Groundwater Awareness Week. Groundwater Awareness Week helps spotlight one of the world's most important issue: groundwater!

At times I felt like the ringmaster in a circus. Inmate Jones was a fifty-year-old black man serving twenty years for kidnapping. Jones sat buck-naked on his sink all day long because he had bad hemorrhoids. Each time I passed his cell he smiled and waved. "We got a biological disaster in my ass!"

Inmate Owens was a black midget, nicknamed "Six Inch." Owens enjoyed singing Madonna songs while standing on his head between the cell bunks. He was twenty-one years old, serving a life sentence for murder. He would hide under the bunk at count time. When I would open the food port, his beady little eyes would dart back and forth like a cartoon character's until he scampered under his bunk. The first time I met him I couldn't find him anywhere inside the cell. The frame of the door blocked my view, but I could hear him singing, "Like a virgin, touched for the very first time!" His wrists were so small that the handcuffs would fall to the floor. I had to escort him to the shower without restraints.

Inmate Wayne was nicknamed "Pigpen." He never came out of his cell when I came around for inmate showers. He liked to sleep on the floor. His cell was filthy, but if I attempted to clean it out, he would throw a fit and cover his cell walls with feces, so I just let him sleep in his own garbage.

"I haven't showered in three months, buddy!" complained Pigpen.

"You just showered ten minutes ago, remember, buddy?"

"Oh, yeah, I forgot. Thanks, buddy."

"Satan is dating Drew Barrymore!"

"If Satan's dating anyone, it's Courtney Love."

"I killed Jimmy Hoffa and the Teamsters are after me!"

"No, you kidnapped Frank Sinatra Jr., don't you remember?"

"My mattress is talking to me."

"Talk back and make friends."

"Good idea. Thanks buddy."

Inmate Downs was a fifty-year-old black man with a full beard who confidently told me every day that he was only eleven years old and shouldn't be in prison. "I'm only eleven years old, Mister! I don't belong here!" Downs was serving a ten-year sentence for armed robbery. He never said anything except that he was eleven years old and children should not be in prison.

Inmate Artie thought he was a dog. He made a bowl out of cardboard, and used newspapers spread on his cell floor as his toilet. He never spoke. He just barked. His bark was so good many officers who didn't know him thought he actually had a dog in his cell. Artie was serving six years for petty theft, with a prior. He had stolen fifty purses from a downtown Los Angeles fashion show.

Inmate Spoon thought he was a ninja trained in Japan to fight vampires. Spoon was twenty-six and had dropped out of school in the ninth grade. He had set his foster brother on fire with a can of gasoline. Spoon tore his jumpsuit and made a karate uniform with a hood. Spoon always spoke about himself in third person. "The white ninja thanks you for this meal," he proclaimed. "Keee-ya!"

Inmate York's nickname was "Spiderman," because he liked to brace himself against the cell walls above the door. York was twenty-three and had been a gymnast in high school. Many officers who weren't familiar with Spiderman assumed he had escaped, because he could not be seen inside the cell unless the door was opened. Spiderman suspended himself above the cell door for hours. York was serving nine years for stabbing a man at a house party.

Inmate Calhoun asked me to teach him algebra one day. Calhoun was thirty-five and had dropped out of school in the sixth grade. He was raised by his grandmother in Watts and never knew his parents. He had been addicted to smoking crack and had lived most of his adult life in homeless shelters. Sergeant Arnold was not happy about me educating the inmates. I would pull up a chair and go over Calhoun's math problems at the food port. I gave him the nickname "Calculus," and soon all the inmates called him that. Someone even put it in his file.

Inmate Charles was dying of liver cancer. He was serving a life sentence for murder, and would go out daily for chemotherapy. Shaking hands with the inmates was frowned upon, but inside Adseg I was free from the critics. I shook Charles' hand each time he came back from the hospital. Charles was one of the inmates who had gotten into a fight on Delta Yard when I was in the control booth. He had called me a motherfucker and promised to kill me when he got out of his cuffs. He was just waiting to die. He woke each day with the intention of staying alive. He was one of the few inmates I cared about.

Inmate Legal Larry filed more than fifty lawsuits against officers for allegedly planting a micro-chip in his brain and recording his phone conversations with the Pope. NASA even wrote him back a letter asking him not to write them any more letters. Larry was serving twelve years for manslaughter; he had run over a woman while drunk. Larry was fifty-two, an aging hippie in the last place he thought he'd ever be.

Inmate Sanchez was the only inmate I ever believed was innocent. He wasn't innocent of the crime, but he was innocent of the charge. Sanchez had been at a theme park with his girlfriend when two gangbangers saw his gang tattoos and attacked him. Sanchez was five-foot-four, and weighed 120 pounds. The two assailants continued to beat Sanchez while he was on the ground. Sanchez pulled a knife from his pocket and sliced both men. The two attackers called the police and testified that Sanchez tried to rob them and used the knife during the robbery. Sanchez allowed me to read his court papers; because Sanchez had prior convictions and he had used a weapon at the time of his arrest, he was charged with attempted murder and struck out under the "Three Strikes" law. Sanchez had defended himself in court. The justice system has nothing to do with right or wrong; it has to do with who has the better attorney, and Sanchez didn't. Sanchez was twenty-seven, serving a life sentence.

Inmate Jack "Elvis" Presley claimed to be the tenth cousin of Elvis Presley. He was twenty-eight and from Tennessee. He loved to sing Elvis songs, and had been an Elvis impersonator on the streets. He was serving three years for check fraud; he had forged his mother's signature so he could buy a guitar. Inmate Presley promised that when he got out, he would give me a job as his body guard, for $5,000 a month plus benefits.

My favorite inmate was Timmy Burrows. Timmy had been a professional golfer. Officer Felix nicknamed him "Tincup." Timmy had started smoking crack and bought a new Chevy Tahoe with a fake check. After the check bounced, the auto dealership called and asked for the car back. Timmy brought it back with the seats ripped out; he'd needed a couch for his apartment. He was given a two-year sentence because at his trial he spat on the judge. Timmy kept his cell dark and none of the officers paid much attention to him. Timmy was twenty-two and had graduated from USC. He was short and thin and could have passed for a high school student. He was from a wealthy family from Orange County and had been in several mental institutions. The FBI showed up one afternoon with several eight-by-ten-inch glossy photos of what appeared to be trash. Timmy had been busy sending actress Tori Spelling love letters. Timmy also sent her a jacket he made out of his prison jumpsuit complete with a heart stitched in the center of it. Timmy mailed it off in a box along with fifty-seven packets of ketchup from the prison kitchen. FBI Special Agent Bryant placed the photos on the table in front of me while I was eating a hamburger in the committee room.

"I'm investigating a stalking case. Do you know why Inmate Burrows would send these items?" asked the FBI agent.

"Yes. He's crazy."

"How do you know?"

"Because he's stalking Tori Spelling."

There was always a dilemma in The Hole when choosing your battles. The one thing I tried not to do was piss off the inmates, because they held grudges. However, there were always inmates I couldn't smother with kindness. Some of them were just angry. A product of severe isolation from the rest of the world.

All of the assaults against me happened while I was working in The Hole. Usually it was something minor, like an inmate verbally threatening my life. People on the outside were always astonished when I told them that the inmates tried to attack the officers.

Legal Larry attacked me one day. He was the last inmate I ever thought would want to harm me, but he just snapped. Larry had sharpened a state-issued toothbrush and slashed himself repeatedly. Over the next several days Larry was taken to the infirmary daily for self-inflicted wounds, and then returned to his cell. "His cutting ritual is his way of getting attention," explained Dr. Colby.

"Yeah, but he cuts himself all the time. That can't be normal."

"We consider his wounds to be superficial."

"He's covered head to toe with scars."

I thought Inmate Larry was a complete nut job, but the medical staff didn't seem to think anything was wrong with him. His cell was cleaned out for any sharp objects, but he continued to find ways to cut himself. Other inmates on the tiers were happy to slide objects like pens and staples under his door.

Inmate Larry wouldn't stop cutting himself no matter what I tried to do. The time finally came for me to give him a shower, because second and third watch rotated tiers during the week.

"Can I get a razor?" Larry asked.

"No."

"Why not?"

"Take a wild guess."

"How am I supposed to shave?" Larry asked.

"You're not. That's what 'razor restriction' means."

"What am I on razor restriction for?"

"The razors are afraid of you."

Larry put his hands through the port and I placed handcuffs on his wrists. The door opened and I escorted him to the shower. He stepped in and I closed the shower door. He turned around and put his hands through the bars and I un-cuffed him. He took a ten-minute shower. When he was done showering, I placed him in handcuffs and waved for the control officer to open the shower door. The shower was on the top tier right next to the inmate's cell. He only had a few feet to go until we reached the door frame.

Larry stepped out and I motioned again to the control officer to close the cell door. Larry looked back at me with hollow eyes and laughed.

"I'm the devil!" Larry screamed.

Larry kicked me in the stomach, knocking me back. If it had been any harder, I would have gone right over the tier. I lunged toward Larry and tackled him around the waist. The impact of our bodies echoed in the cell as we crashed to the floor. I expected Larry to resist and continue to struggle, but he didn't. He went limp. He lay on the cell floor like he was dead.

During Larry's criminal hearing for assault and battery, he denied ever kicking me or even being in the housing unit at the time of the incident.

"I was at home watching TV with my mom," Larry insisted.

At the infirmary Larry was given a shot by Dr. Colby and sedated. He had told another officer that he had swallowed some pills. His heart rate was high and he kept screaming, "I want to die!" A tube was snaked down his throat to pump his stomach. The inmate immediately started to gag and vomit. A multitude of colorful pills came up, pouring out of his mouth in a pool of bile like he was a Pez dispenser.

"Jesus, that must be about a hundred pills," said Dr. Colby.

"I told you," slurred Larry.

"Yes, you did."

It was more pills than I thought humanly possible to consume. Larry groaned and spat out a set of false teeth. Tears started streaming from his eyes when he saw his teeth on the floor.

"Why did you do this to me?" asked Larry. "I thought you were different!"

"I didn't do anything."

Larry was in such a pitiful state that I actually felt sorry for him. It was the first time I had felt deep compassion for an inmate.

But I felt even worse when I read his file and looked into his background. As a child he had been set on fire by his father in a drunken stupor. He still had burn scars on half his body. I had been obsessed with learning the background of every inmate at the prison, but after Larry I realized it only clouded my judgment. I never read another inmate file again.

Attention Staff:
This is National Wolf Awareness Week. It is time to dispel misconceptions about wolves and to teach about the importance and role these animals play in maintaining a healthy ecosystem.

A month later I found myself sitting across from Sergeant Arnold in his office. He had changed positions and was now in charge of institutional training. Each prison had a sergeant who was in charge of making sure each officer was documented on paper as being trained to prison standards. In court the first question a lawyer always asked was, "Who trained you?"

"You're being issued a write-up for not pressing your alarm during that assault on Inmate Larry," said Arnold.

"What? I don't have an alarm. That's ridiculous."

"*You* may find it ridiculous," said Arnold, "but the Review Board does not. This is very serious."

"How can I hit an alarm that I don't have?"

"See, you have to hit your alarm whenever you're in an incident," said Sergeant Arnold.

Arnold didn't even look at me. "You've got to hit that alarm," repeated Arnold. "It's department policy." He slid a document across the desk. "I need you to sign this disciplinary write-up that states you admit guilt in this incident."

"Guilt? What did I do? This is bullshit."

"Watch your language. I'm a Christian. Inmate Larry is a medical inmate. He cannot be held accountable for his actions."

"And what if I don't sign it?"

Arnold raised his eyebrows and looked up at me. "Then you'll be insubordinate. That's another write-up."

I gave up. I knew it was a joke. "We wouldn't want that to happen."

"No, we wouldn't. See, you can't be a cowboy at this institution. You have to follow the rules. We need team players here, not people who go off attacking inmates."

I signed the form just so I could leave. I knew it didn't matter. I had become dumber just listening to Sergeant Arnold.

Attention Staff:
This week is National Eating Disorder Awareness Week. If you know someone with an eating disorder, reach out and help them. Call the eating disorder hotline ASAP. The helpline serves individuals dealing with binge eating and obesity.

Walking through the crowded employee parking lot before shift change, I saw Officer Felix coming toward me. I smiled and waved. He grabbed me and threw me against a car. He dug his hand in the back of my collar. The buttons on my jacket scraped across the hood of the car.

"What the hell are you doing?!"

I pushed Felix back, but he held onto my uniform, patting me down like I was an inmate.

"Where's the wire?" Felix yelled.

"What wire?"

I thought he was joking, but then I looked in his eyes. He was on a mission. This was no joke. He was deadly serious.

"Slow down. What are you talking about?"

"You know what I'm talking about, motherfucker! I can't believe I trusted you. I let you into my life. Jesus, you've been to my house! You've met my wife and kids!"

"I swear to God, I don't know what you're talking about. Who told you this?"

"I know you're internal affairs. I had a dream that you pulled a wire out of your collar. You've been recording us the whole time. You had a wire that you kept in your back."

I pushed him back harder this time until he let go. He was out of breath.

"Listen to yourself," I said. "It was a dream. Dreams aren't real. Get a hold of yourself. You sound like a fucking idiot."

Felix took a deep breath and fell down on one knee. "I'm sorry, man. This whole fucking place has gotten to me!"

"It's all right. Now get up before someone sees you." I extended my hand and pulled him to his feet. Felix grabbed me and gave me a long awkward hug. Felix had always been a loyal employee. The prison tried to burn him, charging him with battery when he defended himself against an inmate attack. The new guidelines made any contact with an inmate a criminal offense. Officer Felix was the first officer to be made an example of by the administration. Sergeant Arnold was trying to get him fired. Felix took leave for stress. I never saw him again.

A few weeks later, the Adseg sergeant was replaced by Sergeant Linden. She had been demoted from lieutenant for stalking Officer Harvey. Linden was not prepared for the amount of work Adseg had to offer. She was also an alcoholic who drank on the job. It was almost like the prison encouraged staff to drink. She was afraid of the inmates. Her voice cracked when she spoke to them. Her favorite line was, "I can handle this, I'm a grandmother!"

The prison policy in The Hole quickly changed from punishing the inmates to punishing the officers. Fridays in The Hole became known as "Fucked-up Fridays" because the inmates wanted to go to the infirmary for the weekend. Before, there had to be a reason to escort an inmate down to the hospital; now, Sergeant Linden just couldn't say no. Most of the time she was passed out in her office or crying.

"We now have to ask the inmates if they want their medication," said Linden. "If the inmate refuses meds and we try to force them on him, we can be charged with battery."

When I first started, if an inmate talked shit, you talked shit back; now they chastised officers for disrespecting the inmates. When an inmate took your cuffs, you got them back; now we had to contact every member of the administration and negotiate with the inmate to get the cuffs returned. When an inmate refused to come out of his cell, you went in and dragged him out; now supervisors bribed and bartered with extra lunches and canteen. When the inmates said they were going to fight, officers said, "Get along or get it on"; now officers had to take the inmates out and separate them. The new policy forced the prison to take away all authority from the officers and handed it over to the inmates.

Officers needed a reason to search the inmates and search their cells. Officers were told not to pepper-spray the inmates, because the inmates had complained that it was inhumane. Officers were blamed when the inmates got in cell fights. Officers were job-changed to please the inmates. Officers were held accountable when the inmates didn't shower or shave. Officer Gump was job-changed when an inmate filed a grievance stating that Gump did not give him an extra piece of bread at dinner.

Supervisors took the word of inmates over officers before they even heard both sides of the story. If an inmate complained about an officer, the complaint was immediately investigated. Administrators believed that an officer must have provoked an inmate into assaulting him; the officers were made out to be the bad guys. A new breed of supervisor had emerged right along with a new breed of inmate.

Attention Staff:
A suggestion box has been placed outside the door of the warden's office located inside the Administration Building. This box is to set up a line of communication between the warden and all employees. Please keep your comments professional.

I was fed up with Adseg, and transferred to Charlie Yard as a control booth officer. I stayed on third watch, with Thursdays and Fridays off, for a year.

I had been married for two years. I came home one evening and felt tension like never before. She was sitting on the couch watching TV and doing her best to ignore me.

"How was your day?" I asked.

"Okay."

"Everything all right."

"Yes."

"Are you sure? Is there something you want to talk about?"

"What has happened to you?"

"What do you mean?"

"You've changed."

"No, I haven't."

"Jesus Christ, you sleep on the couch with a loaded gun!"

It was the most logical place to sleep in the house in case someone tried to break in.

"It's to protect you."

"You pulled a gun on me the other night!"

"I thought you were an intruder."

I was asleep on the couch and when she walked into the room, I panicked. I thought for sure she was going to attack me. I had woken up from another nightmare.

"The gun wasn't even loaded."

"Your job is ruining our marriage."

"What else am I supposed to do?"

"I'm embarrassed to tell anyone that you're a prison guard. I say you're unemployed. My family and friends barely know you. They joke that you're imaginary."

"Who cares what people think?"

"Everyone cares! That's what life is all about! We can't have kids with you working in a prison."

She didn't understand the job. We had agreed to never discuss the prison, and for years it worked; she didn't ask, and I didn't offer. I did a good job of hiding my feelings from my wife. I always left the prison behind, but by my fourth year a deep depression had made a home in my brain. I was plagued with the same problem that other officers had when they wanted to quit: I didn't know where to go next. I was making good money. I had a mortgage and bills to pay. We had car loans and student loans. We were in debt like a lot of other families. I felt like I was on borrowed time. The odds of me getting stabbed to death by an inmate were becoming greater. The stress of prison was getting to me. I wasn't religious, but the prison made me want to pray every night. I wore a silver St. Michael medallion, the patron saint of law enforcement. I carried around a pack of Rolaids and ate them like they were Skittles. Pepto-Bismol and Zantac had become my new best friends. On the floor an officer could burn off calories from walking around, but control booth officers were stuck in one place. I ate junk food and developed a twelve-pack-a-day Mountain Dew habit. I gained so much weight that when I went to put on a suit for a friend's wedding, I looked like Pee-Wee Herman. I had never been more than 190 pounds in my life and now I weighed 230. The only thing that saved me from looking like a total slob was my height, six-foot-two. I was exhausted all the time and I never exercised. I was pale in color. My skin looked sickly. I had headaches and on my days off they got worse knowing that I had to go back to work. I was stuck in a never-ending war zone. I was depressed because all I saw was the evil side of humanity.

When I was off duty I found myself irritated by anyone who didn't listen to me, because my patience had worn thin telling inmates what to do. I challenged anyone who questioned me—a waitress in a restaurant who didn't bring me my exact order, a car driving too slowly on the freeway.

I had a good family and good friends, but they didn't understand the job. They didn't understand me; only other prison guards did. Only prison guards could relate to the stories I was telling about the prison.

After five years as a prison guard, I quit. I turned in my badge to the personnel office. It was tossed into an unmarked drawer with other badges by an unknown clerk. After five years, I was treated just like everyone else. There was no reward for my service. There was no certificate to frame or party to attend. There was no handshake from the warden. No parade. I was just another citizen now. As I exited the office, Sergeant Arnold walked down the hall toward me.

"You need to iron that uniform."

"Fuck off," I said, walking past him.

"What did you say?" he yelled.

"You heard me."

"You come back here!"

ABOUT THE AUTHOR

Mike Knox is a writer, stand-up comedian, and documentary film producer. He lives in Los Angeles.

ABOUT THE PUBLISHER

The Sager Group was founded in 1984. In 2012 it was chartered as a multimedia artists' and writers' consortium, with the intent of empowering those who make art—an umbrella beneath which makers can pursue, and profit from, their craft directly, without gatekeepers. TSG publishes eBooks and paper books; manages musical acts and produces live shows; ministers to artists and provides modest grants; and produces documentary, feature, and web-based films. By harnessing the means of production, The Sager Group helps artists help themselves. For more information, please visit www.TheSagerGroup.net.

www.ingramcontent.com/pod-product-compliance
Lightning Source LLC
Chambersburg PA
CBHW030106260626
47156CB00008B/2551